SUMMER FLIGHT

by

M A R G A R E T   Y O R K E

SEVERN
SH
HOUSE

This 1986 edition from SEVERN HOUSE PUBLISHERS
LTD of
4 Brook Street, London W1Y 1AA
First published in Great Britain 1957 by Robert Hale Ltd.

British Library Cataloguing in Publication Data
Yorke, Margaret
Summer flight.
I. Title
823'.914[F]   PR6075.07
ISBN 0–7278–1367–6

Printed in Great Britain
at the University Printing House, Oxford

SUMMER FLIGHT

The chief event of the August Bank Holiday week-end in Bramsbourne is always the
Annual Fête and Flower Show. But other
occurrences are to make this one particularly
memorable.

As usual, everyone is taking part in the
preparations, and families are gathering from
far and near. At the Priory, Brigadier and
Mrs. Trent welcome their daughter Susan
with her husband and two children, and their
daughter-in-law Elizabeth. Only their son
Victor is absent, a cause for sorrow which by
tacit agreement is not mentioned.

Into this peaceful and expectant scene
comes a man on the run. His efforts to evade
the police net tightening around him affect,
one after another, everyone in the village.
None escapes the consequences of his
presence. But the Trents, and the war-dis-
abled Vicar, are more deeply concerned than
any.

CONTENTS

PART ONE

FRIDAY

I

Rain had fallen during the night and through the morning, but now it had stopped, and the sinking sun shone fitfully from the still clouded sky upon the peaceful village of Bramsbourne. The air smelled damp and fresh, and in cottage gardens people looked anxiously at their roses and gladioli, hoping to find them unharmed by the weather and ready to be worthy challengers at the Flower Show on Monday. Housewives brooded over their pet recipes for cakes, or proudly chose the bottles of fruit and jars of jam on whose merits they hoped to soar to glory; husbands relaxed in their shirt sleeves, savouring the prospect of the long holiday week-end, or slipped quietly down to the Rose and Crown for a pint and a chat; children slept, and dreamed of candy floss and roundabouts.

At the Vicarage, the Reverend Richard Dell, D.S.C., was finishing his sermon in readiness for Sunday morning, so that he would be free tomorrow to devote himself to preparations for the Flower Show which was Bramsbourne's big moment of the year. The exhibits were displayed and judged in a large marquee in the Big Meadow; sports were held for the children, and a travelling merry-go-round spun them about till they and their money were exhausted.

Richard sought, with illustrations from the marriage feast at Cana, to point the virtues of such innocent pleasure. Presently, satisfied, he laid down his pen and put the page of notes into a drawer of the wide flat desk where he sat. The evening was warm, and scents from the orderly garden beyond the open french windows wafted gently into the room. He picked up the

9

pipe which lay forgotten beside him and re-lit it; then, puffing contentedly, he got up and went out of his study into the garden, moving a little stiffly for a man who was not yet forty.

The lawn was neatly mown, and flowers glowed in the bright borders. He limped slowly round, wondering how many would be left after his housekeeper had cut enough for her entries, and deciding which beans and cabbages he could fairly exhibit on his own account without disgracing his reputation and yet without fear of depriving a deserving parishioner of a prize. After three years he still felt guilty at living so peace-fully in this quiet country parish. During the war he had been a chaplain at sea, and after that he had a parish in a busy dockland area, but reluctantly he had been compelled to admit the limitations of his non-existent left leg and seek a living which would make fewer physical demands upon him. Four days in an open boat with his shattered leg crudely bandaged by his companions had not helped the broken muscles and nerves that remained, and he still felt frequent pain, but away from the damp and foggy dockland with its tenement dwellings and steep stairways it ached less; and the pure country air combined with the good cooking of Mrs. Maggs his house-keeper, who had once been his nanny, had helped him to regain a good measure of general health. He was popular in the parish, where the villagers, at first necessarily suspicious of anyone new, now flocked to church in ever-increasing num-bers. Richard spoke to them as he had to his seamen, briefly, in a language they understood, neither beating about his point for twenty minutes nor losing himself in abstruse and scholarly argument. Also the village admired a man who was such a good fast bowler, even with one leg not his own.

"Human, 'e is, parson," they nodded in the Rose and Crown.

"A practical Christian," approved the larger houses, hear-ing how when an emergency had sent the mother of five children into hospital, he had immediately with his own hands finished preparing the meal she had been cooking when she had tipped boiling fat over her leg, fed the children, and then found homes for them with neighbours until their mother had recovered, himself having the father and the youngest child at the Vicarage.

"He'll get them all taking advantage of him," said the cynical, wagging their heads.

Richard knew nothing of these discussions, and if he had would have taken no notice. He merely did what he felt was his duty.

Now he looked doubtfully at the sky, and wondered if a small prayer for a fine week-end would be presumptuous. The weather could make or mar the whole Bank Holiday, and particularly the success of the Flower Show. It was always held at this time, although every year hopeful spirits, mostly growers of roses or chrysanthemums, sought to have it advanced or retarded to favour their specialities. Every year since Richard had been Vicar of Bramsbourne rain had interrupted the sports and sent everyone scurrying and jostling into the marquee for shelter.

Dusk was falling now, and coming towards the house again Richard saw the light burning in the kitchen. He went in by the back door, and beheld his housekeeper Mrs. Maggs busily stirring a large bowl.

"What are you up to now, Maggie dear?" he asked, taking his pipe from his mouth. "It's past your bedtime."

The old woman smiled at him, feeling again the sadness she always experienced when she saw him unconsciously shift his weight on to his good leg, and stand a little lopsidedly to speak to her.

"I'm just running up a nice sponge for Mrs. Trent," she told him. "She's got the house full this week-end and it will be a help to her with the children coming. She's shorthanded with that Marlene away again."

"Oh, dear, not again?" sighed Richard. "The last one's only about six months old, isn't it?"

"Nearly ten, dear, and the new one's due in three weeks," said Mrs. Maggs disapprovingly. "That makes four, and all under five, with a different father for each of them, I shouldn't wonder. I don't know why Mrs. Trent has her back between times, I really don't."

"Oh, well, she's a pleasant, kind-hearted girl, you know, Maggie," said Richard with a smile. "Too kind-hearted, perhaps; she hasn't learned how to say 'no.' Mrs. Trent says she works very hard."

"Well, you'll have to talk to her again after this, Master Dick," said Mrs. Maggs, pouring her bubbly primrose mixture into two round tins. "It's your job to make her see the Error of her Ways," she pronounced, and closed the oven door firmly upon her masterpiece. "Anyway, I have hopes of arranging something for Mrs. Trent. I've heard that Mrs. Meaker is thinking of taking a job. She was a cook before she married, and now her boy's away in the Army she wants something to do. So I'll just mention it to Mrs. Trent when I slip up with the cake in the morning."

"Oh, do that, Maggie," Richard agreed. "It would be a good idea. And it is kind of you to make the cake for them, I know they'll be grateful."

"Poor Mrs. Trent, she has enough to worry about and she's looking very tired," said Mrs. Maggs. "Now not a word about Mrs. Meaker till I've arranged it, mind."

Richard laughed. "Not a word," he promised, and left the kitchen, thinking as he often did that Mrs. Maggs accomplished more than he in oiling the machinery of village life.

A tantalising smell began to come wisping from the oven as Mrs. Maggs piled her bowls and spoon into the sink. She would never grow used to seeing Richard drag that leg along; to her he was still the child she had watched grow from a tiny, dark, often angry baby into a merry little boy with thick brown hair falling into his eyes, and it was difficult to realise he was a grown man. With possessive pride she knew he needed her still, yet she could not last for ever, she was seventy-two, and lately she had become aware of a queer dragging pain in her side that seemed to grow more persistent. It was a pity he hadn't found some nice girl to marry him; still, girls didn't much fancy the life of a parson's wife these days, they were too keen on having a gay time. Someone like Elizabeth Trent would suit him nicely; she was quiet and not too young. Mrs.

Maggs sighed; what a tragic business that was. Well, it was no use brooding over it. She turned on the hot tap and switched her thoughts firmly towards washing-up.

II

At the Priory, half a mile from the Vicarage, Mrs. Trent was making a final tour of the house to be sure that everything was ready for the arrival of her family tomorrow. She was a slender, faded woman in late middle age; her face still showed the beauty of its delicate bone structure, although the soft skin was marred by worried lines about the eyes. She sighed now and then as she moved through the gracious old house, wishing that the happy fact of having one's family around one did not involve quite so much work, and wishing too that she might feel a little less tired and so better able to cope with the demands of the busy week-end.

In the larder a bowl of ready peeled potatoes represented Marlene's last act before her temporary retirement. I shouldn't let her come back, really, I suppose, thought Mrs. Trent ruefully, but she's such a kind creature in spite of her failings, and anyway there's no one else. Mrs. Green can't manage everything alone, and I certainly can't either. Oh dear, what a lot there will be to do this week-end, and the Flower Show as well. Of course the girls will help, but Susan has the children to see to, and Nicholas is still quite a baby. Elizabeth was sure to prove a tower of strength, as always, yet she should relax as much as possible since she so seldom left London. It was good that she was coming; Mrs. Trent felt a little rush of warmth run through her at the prospect.

She went through the hall and walked slowly up the wide staircase, pausing on the landing to look out of the window. In the distance the evening light slanted across the hill, patched with fields of meadowland and corn, that lay. beyond the garden. A cluster of willows bending over the brook marked the southern boundary of the Priory grounds, and on its farther side only a few lonely cottages and clumps of elms broke up the orderly pattern of the fields. The house was a little detached from the village which straggled away to the north.

Soon it would be dusk: Mrs. Trent went on upstairs and into the large spare bedroom where Susan and her husband Hugh would be sleeping tomorrow. It was austerely tidy, the neat twin beds impersonal beneath their smooth spreads, the dressing-table gleaming mahogany, devoid of brush or comb. All would be changed in a twinkling when Susan had flung down her possessions, spilled powder, and left her shoes in different corners of the room, thought her mother with an indulgent smile. She was not much tidier than she had been as a schoolgirl, in spite of being married to a very methodical, slightly pompous husband. She was gay and plump; her children were round and rosy; Hugh was adequately prosperous; she was healthy and happy and had seldom in her life caused her parents a moment's anxiety.

The children would share the former night nursery. The cot for Nicholas waited now in one corner, and Susan's old, cream-painted bed was ready for her daughter. It will be lovely to see the darling children again, thought Mrs. Trent. They cheer us even while they exhaust us; they distract our thoughts from the unalterable past and remind us of the future. For the next three days their pounding footsteps, so far removed in fact from the tiny patterings of the poet, and their clear young voices, would fill the house, blotting out with noise and laughter the unhappiness that was so hard to bury when it was empty.

Mrs. Trent left the night nursery and went on down the landing past her own and her husband's bedroom to the last door at the end of the passage. It opened into a small, bright room overlooking the garden, the brook and the hill. It had been freshly painted and there were new curtains and a bed-spread of yellow chintz patterned with roses. This was Elizabeth's room. I do hope she will like it, thought Mrs. Trent, moving the bowl of flowers on the dressing-table into a better position. London is so tiring in the heat of summer, filled with noise and bustle, dust everywhere; perhaps now that her room had been made so pleasant Elizabeth would come home more often. She took a last lingering look round before she closed the door and went downstairs to the drawing-room. It was getting dark now, and the long windows looked out on to a garden full of mysterious shadows. Under a tall standard lamp Brigadier Trent sat reading *The Times*. He lowered the paper and looked over the top of his spectacles above it as his wife entered the room.

" Everything is ready," she said, " Isn't it nice to think that this time tomorrow the house will be full?"

Her husband grunted. " I rather wish they weren't all coming. It makes a lot of work for you, and there's quite enough already with the Flower Show," he said.

" Nonsense, dear, it's lovely to see them and it does the children so much good to get into the real country, and play, in a big garden." Whatever her secret thoughts, Mrs. Trent was shocked to hear her family described aloud as a nuisance. " Besides, they all help, so it doesn't make much work," she added.

She did not sit down, but moved restlessly about the room, altering the position of ashtrays and ornaments, and looking critically in the half light at her flower arrangements, done today for tomorrow there would be no time, and from flowers picked with care to leave the best for the Show. On the bookcase stood a row of photographs; Susan, taken at the time of her engagement, was plumper now, but otherwise little changed in the nine years that had passed since then; her daughter Julia, prim with pigtails, and Nicholas, strangely tidy in his buster suit, flanked their mother; while a somewhat self-conscious image of Hugh, neatly moustached and with his arms folded, stood a little apart from the rest of his family.

Mrs. Trent looked at them all and then she picked up Elizabeth's photograph from the walnut desk where it stood alone.

" I must get the girls to go and be photographed again," she said, looking at the serene young face with its clear, untroubled expression. " These are so out of date." She carried it to the window and stood looking thoughtfully at it in the dim light.

" I don't know why you bother," said the Brigadier. " They

still look exactly the same, and even if you do have new ones done you'll never bring yourself to put those away."

"Oh, they have changed, George," protested Mrs. Trent. "Not Susan so much, though she's fatter, but Elizabeth is beautiful now, far lovelier than when she was a girl."

"Hm, well, I think those are perfectly all right," said her husband. "I shouldn't waste your money. In any case by the time Julia and Nick are a few years older there won't be room for any more." He spoke truly, for small laughing snapshots in neat little frames stood in every vacant corner, because their grandmother could not bear to hide away such enchanting reminders of the children. Slowly she moved back to her desk to replace the photograph she held, and sighed, remembering the other face which must no longer be exposed to public view, and which sometimes she took from its hiding place to look upon in secret.

PART TWO

SATURDAY

I

It was going to be fine; only the most confirmed pessimist queried the clear blue sky. Richard Dell left the Vicarage early and went down to the Big Meadow. Already the marquee was nearly up, and he was soon busy helping to measure out and rope off the track for the children's sports. He enjoyed the physical activity, and the good company of the men who worked with him. The air was warm and dry, and he scarcely felt his leg as he moved about. Overhead, planes from a nearby R.A.F. aerodrome swooped and screamed as they practised diving through the summer air.

"Can't get used to them jets," said Bert Higgs, landlord of the Rose and Crown and chairman of the Sports Committee, unwinding his huge measuring tape to mark off the hundred yards. "Seems uncanny, if you know what I mean, to see them suddenly appear like that overhead. Then that eerie whistle, just like a soul in torment, begging your pardon, vicar."

Richard laughed. "It is an uncanny noise," he agreed, "and the speed they do, those pilots must have to concentrate every second." He picked up his mallet and began to sink a post into the ground with even, vigorous strokes.

"They're brave lads," assented the landlord. "My Ivy's going steady with one of them. Nice young chap he is, very quiet."

"I've seen him about; Sergeant-Pilot, isn't he?" asked Richard. "He looks a good type. Do you think anything will come of it?"

"Don't know, I'm sure," sighed Bert. "That girl's a real

worry to me. Ever so capable she is, a good little cook and neat in her ways, she'd make any chap a good wife, yet she's got her head full of that film star nonsense. Always reading magazines about them, she is, and putting stuff on her face. I wish to goodness she would settle down, instead of keeping this young fellow on a string."

"I expect it's just growing pains," said Richard soothingly. "She's a pretty girl, and she's had her head turned a bit. She'll forget it all when she's married and got a baby to keep her busy."

"Can't happen too soon for me," said her father worriedly. "Perhaps if her Mum had lived she wouldn't have got like this." He mopped his brow with a large red handkerchief and looked around the field which was rapidly acquiring a business-like appearance. "Maybe it's my fault, letting her get her own way too much."

"I don't think you need blame yourself, Bert," said Richard, stopping his work to look kindly at the heated, anxious man in front of him. "Ivy's a nice girl. She's still very young and she hasn't yet learned to have a sense of proportion; few people of her age have and a lot of girls have far sillier ideas than Ivy. She'll get over it, and if this young man is really fond of her he'll provide her with more to think about than the films."

"She says he's too quiet," grumbled Bert, " and it's true, he is shy, but it's no wonder when she's got her face painted up like a Zulu. That's enough to scare any man."

"Perhaps I could have a word with her," suggested Richard. "She's a valuable member of the choir, and I must say I don't like to see quite so much make-up in church, especially when it's on such a naturally pretty girl."

"Oh, I do wish you would, sir," said Bert gratefully. "She might listen to you. All she says to me is that I don't know what the fashions are. If someone like you who's been about the world tells her off, she'll take notice, I'm sure of that."

Richard patted him on the shoulder. "I won't tell her off," he said, "but I'll tell her how very much prettier she'd be with the colouring God gave her."

II

Nanny Maggs left the Vicarage soon after Richard. In her hand she carried a large cardboard cake box containing the sponge cake. Half way down the village she stopped at a cottage and turned inside. Some ten minutes later she reappeared, smiling, and continued on her way towards the Priory.

Mrs. Trent was in the kitchen, dabbing dripping on the breasts of two plump chickens, when Mrs. Maggs knocked at the back door.

"Oh, come in, Mrs. Maggs," she said. "I am glad to see you. Is this enough, do you suppose, or will they burn? I shall never learn to be a good cook."

Mrs. Maggs advanced into the kitchen and set her cake down upon the table. "I'll just see to those, if you don't mind, madam," she said firmly, taking the baking tin from Mrs. Trent. "I brought a sponge cake for the children, seeing that I know you were shorthanded with that Marlene up to her tricks."

"Oh, Mrs. Maggs, how good of you," exclaimed Mrs. Trent, willingly surrendering the birds to a superior craftswoman. She opened the box and peered in delight at the golden perfection within. "How delicious. They will love it. I'm afraid I'm not much of a cake maker."

"And why should you be, madam, when you haven't been used to it?" demanded Mrs. Maggs, mentally back in 1920. "That's another thing I came to mention. I took the liberty of speaking to Mrs. Meaker, and she'd be very pleased to come here, if you so wish, starting today, to cook lunch, and she'll come back again to cook the dinner for you and the Brigadier, every evening except Sunday and Institute Night." So saying, Mrs. Maggs triumphantly put the chickens, now arranged to her satisfaction, on top of the stove. "There, those are ready," she said. "You won't need to be putting them in the oven just yet."

Mrs. Trent sat abruptly down upon the nearest chair.

"Mrs. Maggs, I can't believe it" she, said.

"She'll be along in half an hour to finish off the lunch, as you'll have Miss Susan and the babies arriving, and to have a chat to settle things," said Mrs. Maggs, well pleased with the success of her role as ministering angel. "I promised to explain first. I hope you don't think me presuming, madam?" she enquired for form's sake.

"Indeed not. I'm incredibly grateful, Mrs. Maggs," said Mrs. Trent with feeling. "It was good of you to think of me. I feel very useless and foolish, not being able to manage better."

"Not at all, madam," said Mrs. Maggs with firmness. "I'm sure I don't see why you should have to when there's no need, and you've never been used to it, and besides you've had enough trouble to bear without the cooking."

Mrs. Trent laughed. Such reasoning, so straightforward to Mrs. Maggs' forthright mind, was yet a little involved. Only she and Richard, in the whole neighbourhood, would have had the courage to refer directly to that unmentionable trouble.

"Elizabeth is coming today as well," she said. "She'll be here in time for lunch."

"Oh, that's nice, madam," said Mrs. Maggs approvingly. "It will do her good to get away from London, nasty dirty, noisy place that it is."

"Yes. But I expect it's best that she should be busy and occupied," said Mrs. Trent sadly.

"Well, maybe it is and maybe it isn't," said Mrs. Maggs ambiguously. "Now, I'd better be off before Mrs. Meaker arrives and finds me still here," she added. "Goodbye, madam."

"Goodbye, Mrs. Maggs, and thank you so much for the lovely cake and for arranging about Mrs. Meaker for me," said Mrs. Trent, getting up from her seat. "I'll see you in church tomorrow, perhaps, or anyway at the Show on Monday."

"Yes, if course, madam. Our runner beans will take a lot of beating," said Mrs. Maggs, and away she went down the drive, well pleased with her morning.

III

Elizabeth Trent sat squeezed into a corner seat in the crowded train. Paddington had been a seething mass of holiday-making travellers, all marvelling at the rare prospect of fine weather. She had been very lucky to get a seat at all, and now she was content, wedged between the window and a sticky child licking an even stickier lollipop, watching the houses rush past, until at last the green fields and winding country roads replaced them. She looked extremely elegant, a slender young woman dressed in a well-cut grey flannel suit and a crisp white blouse. She was the Feature Editor of a woman's magazine.

It was hot in the compartment, and presently she took off her small straw hat and ran her fingers through her short dark curly hair. Gazing at the countryside sweeping past the window, she began to think with pleasure and gratitude of the welcome that awaited her, and the comfort of the lovely old house. As always, it would be peaceful, even with the rowdy company of Julia and Nick. You could relax and stop being efficient or business-like; you could wear old clothes and have untidy hair and bare legs; you did not sleep in a queerly furnished bed-sit. with the noise of traffic thundering outside, but instead you lay between soft old linen sheets that smelled faintly of lavender, with only the sound of the brook and the birds outside. She sighed with pleasure at the prospect of three whole days of contentment. Lunch today would be very noisy, with Susan gaily relating all that had happened since their last meeting and recounting the pranks of Nick and the prowess of Julia, while the men of the family would go into a depressed huddle about income tax and bad driving on the roads. Julia would act the heavy elder sister to Nick, scolding him if he behaved badly, and showing off on her own account. If it stayed fine they might go for a walk over the hill in the afternoon, and later she would help Susan to put the children to bed. After dinner they would probably play Canasta, or perhaps they would simply just talk. It would all

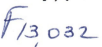

be so perfect, so unchanging, and she would find it hard to leave on Tuesday. One reason why Elizabeth returned to Bramsbourne so seldom was because she could not face the thought of leaving it again.

Tomorrow morning Nick and Julia would come creeping into her bedroom early, as they always did, for a game and a story before breakfast. Then, at last she allowed the thought, there would be church and she would see Richard. Even though he would be surpliced and remote, he would still be Richard, unchanging and unchanged. She let herself remember for a moment their last meeting on the hill at Easter-time; then, with an effort of will she turned her thoughts in another direction.

On Monday there would be the Flower Show. That was always fun, except for the hazard of the weather. Everyone took it so seriously, their whole year ruined if past honours were not upheld. This time Bramsbourne was firmly on the map, for Harley Darrell, the well-known film star, was coming to present the prizes. That would cause a flutter in the female bosoms, reflected Elizabeth with a smile, although by now he must be nearly fifty. No doubt he would be invited to the fork luncheon at the Priory which annually spanned the interval between the morning judging of entries and the official opening ceremony in the afternoon. Richard would be at the luncheon too; once more her thoughts threatened to turn away from control, and she picked up her newspaper to direct them towards more prosaic affairs.

Mrs. Trent was at the station to meet her. They kissed warmly, and went out into the yard where the car was parked. Soon they were driving away, through the outskirts of the town into the country.

"How good it smells," said Elizabeth contentedly. She looked out of the car window at the leafy hedges and the green meadows, punctuated here and there by yellowing fields of corn.

"The harvest will be late this year," said Mrs. Trent. "The corn is only just beginning to turn. We've had such a lot of rain this summer, but it has kept the gardens fresh and green."

She swerved back on to the crown of the narrow lane they were travelling along, having been so busy watching the scenery with Elizabeth that she had scraped against the grass verge. She was no better as a driver than she was as a cook.

They passed a farm, quiet and sleepy in the hot summer day, except for several chickens who ran squawking away from the car. Elizabeth let out a breath of relief when she saw that there were no casualties.

"I always think hens are such silly creatures," observed Mrs. Trent, quite unperturbed. She blew the horn loudly and unnecessarily at a mother who was calmly wheeling a pram along very close to the hedge; the young woman looked round in surprise as the small car went modestly past at twenty miles an hour. Luckily Mrs. Trent always travelled so slowly that there was little fear of her lack of skill causing disaster, unless through making faster traffic impatient.

Further on, they came up behind a large and very smelly converted bus which was proceeding jerkily along the road giving out noxious fumes from the rear. Mrs. Trent tooted her horn at it, but in vain, for there was no room in the narrow lane to pass. A large tin chimney from which came more black smoke was let into the roof of the conveyance; and several dirty children hung out of the open back window making faces at the two women in the car. A smell of frying sausage mingled with the aroma of petrol fumes and oil, and was wafted unpleasantly back by the wind of their progress. As they went round a bend, Elizabeth could see in front of the bus-cum-caravan a large lorry of the type used by fair-men to transport their roundabouts and sideshows.

"It must be the merry-go-round coming up for the Flower Show," said Mrs. Trent. "They're early. Usually they arrive magically in the middle of the night."

"Perhaps they're going to another village first," suggested Elizabeth. "It isn't very likely that they'd miss the chance of a Saturday night stop, is it?"

"I expect you're right. I believe there is a fair at Dimbleton tonight, they must be going there." Mrs. Trent changed gear with a jerk and a grind, resigned to creeping indefinitely behind the cavalcade.

"What a fearful smell," she said. "I suppose they must cook their lunch some time, but it does seem rather strong."

"Mm, yes," agreed Elizabeth. "I wonder what it's like, living in a caravan like that. It must be a hard life, always on the move."

"Yes. One wonders why they do it," said Mrs. Trent.

"I expect they like it. They probably think a settled home is very dull," suggested Elizabeth.

Presently the lorry and the caravan turned off, and Mrs. Trent was able to accelerate and so travel the last few miles at a less snail-like pace. She stalled the engine of the car as she turned in at the Priory gate, however eventually they stopped safely outside the front door.

"Come along, my dear," said Mrs. Trent. "Let's take your things upstairs before Susan and her zoo descend upon us." She got stiffly out of the car, and Elizabeth picked up her suitcase to follow her into the house.

The familiar smell of old furniture, beeswax and flowers greeted her inside the hall, and already the house began to wrap its atmosphere of calm about her.

"Don't bother to come up with me, Mother," she said. "I'll just change and then I'll come and help with the lunch."

"There's no need!" Mrs. Trent's triumph was glorious. She lowered her voice. "There is a Cook in the kitchen," she announced.

The effect was all that she could wish. "Never!" exclaimed Elizabeth. "How marvellous! Where did you find her? And will she stay?" she asked.

"She's daily," Mrs. Trent qualified, "It's Mrs. Meaker. She was a cook before she married." She went on to explain how Mrs. Maggs had made the arrangements.

"Oh, how splendid, and she's such a nice woman, of course I remember her," said Elizabeth. "I'm so glad. Now you'll be able to take things more easily."

"I must admit it is a relief," Mrs. Trent confessed. "It's

going to make so much difference, especially with Marlene away again."

"Oh, not again! How many will this be?" asked Elizabeth.

"I daren't contemplate," laughed Mrs. Trent. Already the presence of Elizabeth was having its usual effect upon her; she felt calmed and happy. She longed to see the girl's reaction to her freshly decorated bedroom, and began to lead the way upstairs.

Elizabeth's response was instant.

"Oh, you've had it painted! And new curtains! Aren't they pretty, and a new dressing-table too! Oh, you do spoil me!" Impulsively she hugged the older woman. "It's perfectly lovely," she said.

Mrs. Trent cleared her throat. "I'm glad you like it, my dear," she said. "It gave me so much pleasure to do it."

"I shan't be able to keep away," cried the girl, putting her hat and gloves down on the bed. "Oh—not that I would only come home to sleep in this lovely room, you know how much I love coming," she added hastily.

"I wish you would come oftener, Elizabeth," said Mrs. Trent. "We're quite different when you're at home. Alone we're very dull old people."

"You'll never be that," said Elizabeth firmly. "And you know, I only stay away because I can't bear to leave."

"But why should you leave?" said Mrs. Trent eagerly. "Why not give up your job and come home for good?"

Elizabeth looked at her seriously. "You know I can't do that," she said quietly. "How could we ever manage if I did?" She turned away and lifted her suitcase on to a chair.

Mrs. Trent raised her hands helplessly for a moment, and then let them fall. This was the remote, dedicated Elizabeth who filled her with awe. She was relieved to hear the sound of a motor horn in the lane outside.

"Oh, that will be Susan and the children," she cried.

Elizabeth looked up then with her gentle smile. "I'll follow you down, Mother," she said. "And thank you again for making my room so lovely."

Mrs. Trent hurried downstairs. Hugh's sleek car was now drawn up on the gravel sweep outside the front door, beside her own more humble model, discharging its cargo of noisy children, one spaniel and two exhausted parents.

Left alone, Elizabeth quickly pulled a cotton dress over her head and ran a comb through her hair. She slipped her feet into light sandals and then went downstairs.

The first greetings were over and the house was now transformed. Julia ran all over it immediately, to make certain that it was just as she remembered, dragging the stout Nicholas in her wake. Susan was pouring out to her mother a dramatic account of the hazards of their journey, how every traffic light had been red and how other evil users of the road had caused them narrowly to miss death several times. The spaniel, liberated at last from his cramped corner in the car, now dashed round the house too, skidding on rugs and scrabbling on the polished floor. Hugh, having greeted his mother-in-law affectionately, disassociated himself from the tumult and began methodically unloading the car.

"Heavens, Susan," exclaimed her mother, "do you really need all that luggage just for three days?"

"Oh, the children would bring nearly every toy they possessed," cried Susan. "I'm worn out. Nick was sick and he just missed my new frock. I suppose I'd better go and see what those two hooligans are up to."

"I'll go if you like, Sue," offered Elizabeth. She adored her niece and nephew and seized every chance for their company, but she feared to be guilty of that common failing of aunts, interference.

However Susan was only too pleased to relinquish some of her responsibility for a time. "Oh, do, Elizabeth, you are an angel," she said gratefully. She followed her mother into the drawing-room, still talking hard to make up for lost time, and Elizabeth tracked Nick and Julia down to the kitchen where they were interested spectators of Mrs. Meaker dishing up the chickens. She bore them away to be washed and tidied for lunch, which was just as noisy and cheerful as she had expected. Nicholas upset his plate all over the floor, but luckily Rusty, the spaniel, who was accustomed to such convenient accidents, was near, waiting hopefully, and he licked up most of the mess.

Julia primly related her latest achievements at school. She was a solemn-looking child with her round face and two long plaits. Elizabeth wished Susan would have them cut, for she thought the little girl would look much prettier with short hair. She took a lot of rousing from her primness, perhaps inherited from Hugh's somewhat heavy manner, but when roused she was delightful, full of fun and given to making shrewdly comic remarks.

Ater lunch Hugh and the Brigadier went off to walk round the garden and attend to other manly affairs.

" I expect they'll end up by having forty winks in Daddy's study," said Susan from long experience. The children, Julia with many shamed protestations, were made to lie on their beds " to rest after the journey," but really in order to give their elders some respite.

Susan flopped into an armchair in the drawing-room.

" Oh, it's nice to sit down," she exclaimed, oblivious of the fact that she had been sitting all morning, first in the car and more recently in the dining-room. " I hear you've got Harley Darrell coming on Monday, Mummy," she said. " What a feat, however did you capture him?"

" Lady Faversham arranged it," said Mrs. Trent. " He's a friend of hers."

" Goodness, is he English, then?" asked Susan. " I always thought he was an American. How I long to meet him, he's so attractive. Don't you think so, Elizabeth?"

" Well, yes, in a way I suppose he is," said Elizabeth with a smile. " As a matter of fact I have met him."

" Have you really?" Susan was impressed.

" Yes, at one or two cocktail parties. He's very nice," Elizabeth told her.

" Girls, you both sound like Ivy Higgs, who's so film-struck that she'll probably faint when she sees him," said Mrs. Trent reprovingly.

" Well, Mummy, you must let us have our day-dreams,"

said Susan, laughing. Mrs. Trent frowned at her, and guiltily she looked at Elizabeth, who merely smiled.

"I have my day-dreams too, Mother," she said gently.

Susan got up impulsively and crossed the room to kiss Elizabeth heartily. "You're nothing short of a saint, Elizabeth," she said, "I'm sorry, but one's bound to mention it some time. I'm a blundering ass, but one can't see all ways round a remark. Forgive me."

"Of course, Sue, don't think about it," said Elizabeth colouring. "I'd much rather discuss it sometimes than have everyone afraid of mentioning it, only I know Father doesn't feel like that. Besides, it's as bad for both of you as it is for me, so why should I be the one to mind?" She smiled, and her face was singularly sweet in its delicate beauty.

"It hasn't wrecked our whole lives like it has yours," said Susan gruffly. She was back in her own chair now, calm restored after her small display of emotion. "But you're right. A skeleton in the cupboard is far more horrifying than one that is brought into the open."

Mrs. Trent looked nervously towards the window; male voices could be heard in the garden as their owners strolled in the direction of the house. "Well, don't let's bring it out just now, Sue," she warned. "It's a lovely day, we ought to be out in the sun instead of sitting indoors."

"It's too hot outside," said Susan lazily, stretching out her sturdy legs in front of her.

Mrs. Trent glanced at her watch. "Goodness, it's getting on for three o'clock already," she exclaimed, and then with a start, "I've forgotten the church flowers! It's my turn this month."

"I'll do them, if you like," Elizabeth offered, getting up from her chair. "I should like to. You and Sue have a nice cosy gossip. What may I take?"

"Oh, would you really do them, Elizabeth? That would be kind," said Mrs. Trent gratefully. "You can pick anything except the delphiniums, or the gladioli or the roses. We need those for the Show."

Elizabeth looked enquiringly out of the open french window

at the wide border which stretched away from the house. "Then it will have to be marguerites," she said. "I'll get the gardening scissors."

Susan glanced at her mother as Elizabeth left the room. The masculine voices had grown fainter now, as the Brigadier, in compliance with Susan's guess, took Hugh into his study.

"Don't you ever talk about it, Mummy?" she asked incredulously.

Mrs. Trent shook her head. "Not since the day when she told us what she was going to do," she answered. "Though we almost did this morning when I suggested she should give up her job. I just daren't contemplate the future, and I don't know how she can face it."

"I don't suppose she thinks about it either," said Susan shrewdly. "I expect her job helps her to concentrate on other things. Poor Elizabeth. Perhaps she'll change her mind eventually."

"I doubt it," said Mrs. Trent. "People like Elizabeth don't change their minds."

Out in the garden, unaware that she was being discussed, Elizabeth moved along the border, selecting her blooms from the shadiest corners, for with the sun beating down on them it was not the best moment to gather flowers. She was glad of the chance to be alone for a while, for the sudden pitchforking into the bustle of the family was a trifle overwhelming. There was a lovely fragrance from the flower beds, and everything shimmered in the heat of the summer sun that was so seldom bold enough to burn. She enjoyed the faint movement of the trees rustling their leaves in the almost still air, and the quietness. Carrying her flowers, she wandered down to the brook and stood watching the water trickling gently along between the narrow banks on its way to the river. Tomorrow she and the children would come and sail twigs and leaves downstream, watching them ride on the current under the bridge and away out of sight. No, certainly she could never agree to abandon her job and live here permanently. If she did that her resolve would weaken and she would never find strength to carry out her chosen task when the time came. It would not be so difficult to quit London. She shuddered as if a cool breeze had blown upon her, and turned her thoughts away from something she could not bear to contemplate; then she went back through the garden and on to the road.

The church lay at the further end of the village, and Elizabeth did not hurry as she walked towards it, enjoying the placid country scene. The cottage gardens were ablaze with colour; full-blown rambler roses hung from every fence; marigolds and petunias shone in bright patches against the darker earth.

There was no one about on this holiday afternoon, except Ivy Higgs and her airman who were waiting for the bus outside the Rose and Crown. Ivy wore a white dress with a scarlet belt, high-heeled toeless sling-back shoes, transparent white lace gloves and a large picture hat ornamented with roses. Her lips were a wide slash of crimson in a face that was smothered with heavy tan make-up, and her long dark hair curled on her shoulders. By her side the young airman seemed very pink and scrubbed; he looked somewhat bewildered, as well he might, to find himself with so exotic a companion. Elizabeth thought he appeared to be a nice sober sort of boy, and marvelled at his courage in escorting Ivy. It was a pity she had grown up into this lurid creature; only a few years ago she had been an unspoilt, natural little girl, well-mannered and unassuming; one could not imagine her now settling happily to the daily routine of the stove and the sink.

After the heat outside it was cool in the old church. Worn by the tread of centuries of worshippers, the stone floor was smooth beneath Elizabeth's sandals. The Norman arch at the transept curved over her head, unchanged since the day long lifetimes past when its last stone had been placed; and on the old oak pews were carved initials and dates that had been inscribed generations ago. It was infinitely calming to be in a building so enduring, that watched endlessly the coming and going of countless people, yet remained constant in itself, an unchanging witness.

Elizabeth moved to the altar and took from it the heavy brass vases. She wrapped last week's faded flowers in an old newspaper, and took the vases outside to rinse and re-fill them. She was back at the altar, absorbed in arranging the tall daisies she had picked when Richard came quietly into the church from the vestry. The afternoon sun slanting through the long windows dappled her dark head with glowing colours from the stained glass. She was slight and lovely, and her task was a graceful one; he watched her with pleasure for some minutes, then, fearing she would turn and see him staring at her, he went to his prayer desk for the book he had come to fetch. Hearing a footstep, Elizabeth looked round. With gladness she recognised Richard, and he came to help her clear up the broken pieces of stem and leaf she had not used.

"How are you, Elizabeth?" he asked.

"Oh, very well. And you?" She smiled at him. "You're very brown."

"It's all the cricket," he told her solemnly. "Every Saturday when fine."

"And how often has that been?" she enquired with a small laugh.

Richard grinned. "Not very often," he admitted, and then, "The flowers look nice."

"I'm afraid they're rather unassuming, only daisies. Everything else is being kept for Monday," she said. "Is that very wrong and shocking?"

"Well, I should have thought it strange to see the best gladioli here," he answered. "Though perhaps they could have been taken out again on Monday morning." They smiled together, old friends happy to be again in each other's company.

"I love this church," said Elizabeth softly as they went back together down the aisle. "It's so old and calm, it makes you feel at peace."

He nodded, and said, "Yes, it's full of gentle ghosts."

They walked slowly round it, looking at the inscriptions on the ancient walls and admiring the ornately carved cover to the font, postponing the moment of parting. Then at last they moved out into the warm sunlight of the churchyard and Richard closed the heavy door behind them.

"I do believe it's going to stay fine," said Elizabeth, looking at the sky. "I hope it will last till after Monday."

"I really think it may, this time," said Richard optimistically, looking at the young woman beside him and not at the blue above.

"I expect you're very busy arranging everything," she said.

"Well, we've done as much as we can until Monday, now," said Richard. "I haven't done too badly; I've learned to delegate my authority," he added with a laugh.

"Your dear Maggie has fixed Mrs. Meaker up to help at the house," said Elizabeth.

"Yes, she told me. I'm glad it all fitted in," said Richard. "Mrs. Trent has been looking very tired lately."

"Yes. I do worry about her," confessed Elizabeth. "Sue can't come down very often with Hugh and the children to cope with, and it makes me feel I ought to; but if I do it will only make it much harder for us all when I can't any more. At least, it would for me," she amended, "but perhaps I shouldn't think of that if it would be better for them?" She looked up at him questioningly, waiting quietly for his advice and wanting to relinquish for a moment her burden of responsibility.

"How can I advise you, dear Elizabeth?" he said. "As a man I should say come home, and give up your plans for the future, but as a priest I know you're right and that you should stick to what you've decided to do. And if you come home, although you will be a comfort and solace to the Trents now, they will miss you even more when you have to go away." He sighed. "What a rotten parson I am," he said bitterly. "Unable to help the one person who is in a real mess, and whom I most want to help."

Elizabeth laughed then. "Oh, Richard, don't be silly, look at what you've achieved since you've been here! You're a first-class parson. Besides, you have helped me, more than I can ever thank you for, just by understanding and not trying to persuade me, and, oh well, being such a good friend." She coloured a little. "It seems to me that the things we most want to do are nearly always wrong, so we should make up our minds to take the least pleasant of any alternatives."

"That certainly seems to be true about this business," said Richard grimly. "It would be wonderful if you did come home, Elizabeth."

"Yes," she said softly. "But it would make it all too difficult. It isn't just because you're a clergyman."

"I know," he said. He stood watching her with great tenderness.

She hesitated, and then said with a rush, "Anyway, it's wonderfully comforting to know that it means the same to you as it does to me. I often remember the things we said that day up on the hill, and it makes me feel glad, and not lonely any more. It's funny, but now that there's so much reason to wish the future need not happen, I feel so much better able to bear it." She smiled then, and added, "We've got a whole weekend now, let's forget our troubles and enjoy it."

He smiled back. "Yes, we will," he agreed. "We'll concentrate our energies on the rival merits of the Priory and the Vicarage runner beans."

Elizabeth laughed. "I must go now, Richard," she said. "They'll wonder where I am."

"I suppose you're all going to the Favershams' cocktail party tonight?" asked Richard as they moved towards the gate.

"The others are going," said Elizabeth. "I promised to stay behind with the children."

"Would you really rather not come? Maggie would come and sit with the children if you like," he said.

"That's kind of you, Richard, but I'd really rather stay at home with the wireless and a book," said Elizabeth. "It will be very hot and noisy at the party, and I shall be much more peaceful."

Richard laughed. "You're absolutely right," he said. "Well, enjoy your rest."

She nodded. "Have a good time at the party," she said with a smile.

Their ways divided at the gate. Elizabeth returned to the

c

Priory, while Richard made his way back to the Vicarage. His heart was heavy; he felt humbled and inadequate.

IV

The inside of the battered caravan that had delayed Mrs. Trent and Elizabeth on their journey from the station was just as smelly as its wake. No one was sorry when Mum, who was at the wheel, blew three blasts on the rasping old horn to inform Dad in the lorry in front that dinner was ready. They stopped on the wide grass verge at the side of the road, all glad of the opportunity to rest, for they had been travelling since first light. Dad, who was the management, clambered nimbly down from the lorry. He had twinkling light blue eyes in a brown face which owed as much of its colour to grime as to the weather. A grubby handkerchief was knotted round his neck; his hair hung picturesquely below his ears, needing the attentions of Mum's cutting-out scissors. He looked enough to frighten any young girl on a dark night, but in reality he was an ardent family man, devoted to the tribe of children and adolescents, all, if not his own, related in various ways to his wife or himself, and relatively faithful.

A tall, thin young man, also rather dirty, followed him out of the lorry. They had picked him up early this morning, hitch-hiking outside Gloucester.

"Come on, mate, there's plenty for you," urged Dad hospitably, offering him a plate of sausage and bacon swimming in fat. "I bet you're hungry; we are, been travelling since dawn, we have."

The young man accepted the food with murmured thanks, and began to eat ravenously. From time to time he looked sharply about him as if he expected to see something. He did not speak. Dad took a shrewd glance at him.

"Like a job of work tonight?" he offered, good-naturedly cuffing one of the children who had tipped its plate of food over his shabby trouser leg. "I expect a busy evening at Dimbleton; we could do with someone to work the motor, while I take the money. The way you fixed the lorry this morning when we picked you up, you must be a bit of a mechanic, eh?"

"Er, yes, I used to be," said the man. "That wasn't much, though, only a bit of faulty wiring."

"I never was no hand at the mechanics," mourned Dad. "Make my job much easier if I was. Young Alfie's a good boy, he's learning, but he ain't got the experience yet." He nodded towards a gangling youth who chewed a huge hunk of bread and cheese, whilst with his spare hand he solemnly polished the bonnet of the bus. It looked no better when he had finished, but Alfie was undismayed. He grinned in a friendly fashion at the stranger, who said, "'Fraid I can't help you tonight, though thanks all the same. Got something fixed already. I'd have been glad to otherwise."

"Oh, that's all right, I just thought it might have done you a good turn," said Dad. He speared a bulging sausage on his fork and stuffed it into his mouth, eyeing the young man speculatively as he slowly chewed.

"Where are you going after Dimbleton?" asked the young man.

"Got a pitch at a place called Brambsbourne for Monday, Flower Show they're having, and rides for the kiddies." He sniffed. "Don't suppose there'll be much profit there."

"Bramsbourne, eh?" said the stranger thoughtfully. "Where do you go after that?"

"Oh, we'll pull out in the night, I expect, or at dawn, and head north; there's a fair up at Noddleburgh the next weekend we've a pitch for. Why? Like to come?"

"I might, if your offer'll hold until then," said the man slowly. "Will it do if I meet you on the road north out of Bramsbourne, before daylight?"

"Not too anxious to be seen, are you?" said Dad with a sly look. "All right—" as the stranger tensed—"Keep your hair on. I don't ask no questions, then I don't know no answers, see?" He lifted his steaming mug of tea to his lips and drank noisily, wiping his mouth afterwards with the back of his oily hand and transferring a fresh smear to his face. He sighed with satisfaction. Mum, a stout woman now, though once she had been alluring as the flexible " Spineless Wonder," handed their guest a mug.

" Drink up," she said, giving him a hearty smack on the back. " A good mechanic's always worth his keep, even if he has got a snappy haircut like yours." She picked up the worn cap which the stranger had laid on the grass beside him. " You should keep it covered up," she said cheerfully. The young man seized it from her hand and pulled it over his close cropped head; a scowl transformed his handsome face before he too attacked his tea.

V

Sergeant-Pilot Alan Blake and Miss Ivy Higgs of the Rose and Crown spent Saturday afternoon in a punt on the river. Ivy reclined gracefully against the shabby cushions, twining her hat ribbons round one hand, and trailing the other in the murky river water, as she had seen Delia Dymple doing in *Yours Till Time Stops* only last week. Her face was expressionless, too stiff beneath its heavy coating of cream and powder to risk the creasing of a smile. Her large dark eyes were discontented, restlessly looking about her, forever seeking the admiration on which she fed. Her full lips drooped sulkily. If only someone important would notice me, she was thinking, a millionaire, or a talent scout; as though such people were likely to be peering from behind the willows on the bank.

She knew very well that Alan was a " good boy," but like many virtues he was dull. He would pop the question in a twink, at the least encouragement from her. Too good to be true, he was; she liked a bit of he-man stuff herself, like Harley Darrell in *The Fighting Females,* dressed as a pirate and carrying off Delia Dymple in a fit of whirlwind passion. The unfortunate Alan, with his tunic off and his shirt sleeves rolled up, looked anything but swashbuckling. His face was red with heat and effort; he was unskilled at paddling a punt; to him the heavens were an easier highway than the river. He was an unhappy young man, for he could think of no way to break through the barrier of what seemed to him to be

Ivy's sophistication. Sometimes he decided that it was not worth even trying, but he could not make up his mind to give her up. Always he returned as a moth to the flame, to be singed afresh.

Lolling in the sun, Ivy half closed her eyes and pretended that Harley Darrell, in a leather jerkin open to reveal his bare muscular chest, was her companion. Dizzily she imagined him sweeping her to him in a fierce embrace, loudly declaring his passion and swearing he would gladly die for her. Alan would never have the nerve to sweep her to him in a fierce embrace, she thought scornfully, he'd never done more than hold her hand at the flicks.

Presently her bashful suitor said, " Shall we tie up for a bit, Ivy? There's a nice tree over there." He waved at the left bank, where graceful willows bent long boughs over the water.

" I don't mind, I'm sure," said Ivy in an ungracious voice. Then, because at heart beneath her foolishness she was really a nice girl, she softened enough to say, " Yes, p'raps it would be nice. You must be hot." Alan swelled with joy at these unexpectedly gentle words, and at the smile she gave him even though it made her face crack. Such rare moments made amends for all her tantrums. He manœuvred the punt beneath the shade of the tree. A curtain of slender leaves screened their retreat; he secured the painter to a stout branch, and then boldly moved aft to rest nearer to his goddess.

" That's ever such a pretty frock you're wearing, Ivy," he began tentatively. She preened herself. Alan modestly averted his eyes from her plunging neckline which seemed to him to plunge a little too far. She would have been amazed if she had known the thoughts that were going through his head, so wild that he was shocked at himself.

" I've got a much nicer one for the Flower Show on Monday," she told him, unbending. " Yellow, it is; made of sprigged organdie. Ever so chick. Harley Darrell is coming, you know," she added, uttering the magic name casually as though encounters with such folk were an everyday matter to her.

Even Alan knew who Harley Darrell was, for had not Ivy

raved about him all through their fish and chips after the film last week?

"Oh, er, really?" he said inadequately.

"Yes. I'm quite certain he'll pick me to star with him in his next film," said Ivy confidently. "When he sees me, that is."

Alan saw incredulously that she really believed what she said.

"But would you want to?" he asked in amazement.

"Why, what do you take me for?" she exclaimed. "Think of it, a mink coat and a lovely house with a swimming pool, a big car—" she waved her hand airily. "I'd be famous," she cried.

Alan was appalled. Since she seemed so lovely to him it was clearly possible that Harley Darrell might choose her as a star. In Hollywood they would teach her how to paint her pretty face so that its camouflage didn't show so much, he thought miserably. Despair spurred him on to say, "But Ivy, I was hoping you might, that is—perhaps—one day—we might —get married?" His ears, aghast, heard the rash words of his mouth.

Ivy went off into a peal of laughter.

"What! Do you think I'd marry you?" she exclaimed cruelly. "You must be mad."

Alan hung his head.

"If you don't go to Hollywood," he muttered.

Ivy went on laughing. If Alan had taken a leaf out of Harley Darrell's book and kissed her soundly then and there, much that was to follow would have been avoided. Though she would have protested at first, in the end she would have been moved by his young ardour. But instead he said sheepishly, "I'm sorry, Ivy, I didn't mean to ask you yet."

"Well, whenever you asked me, the answer would have been just the same," said Ivy heatedly. "Do you think I want to waste my youth washing up and having kids and getting old and ugly before I must? Well, you've got another think coming. And if I did want to do that, I'd choose someone with a bit more dash than you've got, Alan Blake, let me tell you.

Why you haven't got the spirit to squash a beetle, let alone fly an aeroplane, I can't think how you managed to get those wings."

For once she had gone too far, touching on what was to Alan sacred ground, his new-won mastery of the air. His face went dark, and for a moment even Ivy was apprehensive. Then he moved and began to untie the boat.

"We'd best be getting back," he said stiffly.

In silence he paddled to the landing stage and returned the punt to its owners. Ivy preceded him in what she hoped was an austerely dignified manner up the steps that led from the river bank to the road, and unhappily they made their way to Pam's Pantry for tea before the cinema. The cynical waitress who served them and who was a student of human nature watched them plough steadily and unspeakingly through two large ham salads, and told her friends in the kitchen that the young lad at table six was tiring of his fancy bit at last.

But in the softening atmosphere of the cinema, Ivy felt ashamed of her outburst, and Alan's anger began to melt. Soon their two shapes merged into one queer bear-like silhouette as they joined hands and leaned against one another in the darkness.

VI

P.C. Hopkins, whose task in life was to protect the inhabitants of Bramsbourne from evildoers, was enjoying a doze on Saturday afternoon. His tunic was off, his shirt was unbuttoned at the neck, and the sporting page of the *Daily Express* was laid across his ample stomach. He breathed heavily. Suddenly his calm was shattered by the ringing of the telephone. The rhythm of his snores ceased abruptly and he sat up with a jerk. Rubbing the sleep from his eyes and blinking, he shuffled, far from alert, across the room to the instrument.

"Yes, yes, Hopkins here," he said irritably, and then respectfully, "Oh, yes sir, yes sir, I'm sorry, sir" and stood to attention though there was no one to witness it, with the receiver to his ear.

Crackle, crackle, crackle, went the voice at the other end, and "Yes sir, yes," went P.C. Hopkins. "No sir, Nothing's been reported," he added, "I see, sir, very good thank you, sir."

He put the telephone back on its hook. Visibly he swelled with importance as he put on his tunic once again. Ponderously he moved to fetch his helmet from the hall stand.

"Daisy!" he roared to Mrs. Hopkins who was busy mixing her caraway cake for the Flower Show. "I 'ave to go hout On Duty. Can't say for sure when I'll be back, but you'll find me in the village should anything arise to need My Attention." Majestically he trod to the shed where lived his bicycle, so frail a steed for such a mighty form. With slow dignity he mounted, and pedalled solemnly away in the direction of the village.

He was having a cup of tea at the post office when Elizabeth walked past on her way back from the church, and he was admiring a giant vegetable marrow in Mrs. Meaker's cottage garden when Hugh's sleek green car sped down the road later in the evening, taking its load to the cocktail party. Clearly P.C. Hopkins was working very hard.

VII

Elizabeth prolonged the bathing of Nick as long as she could. They blew bubbles, and sailed the soap dish, and played with his large red fish. Unusually clean, he looked angelic sitting in the water, soft and round and pink, with his damp hair curling above his impish face. Wrapped in a fluffy white towel on her lap, he was a cuddly bundle being jiggety-jogged to market. He thoroughly enjoyed being the centre of attraction and laughed with delight as his aunt bumped him up and down, and counted his toes and tickled him.

"Me like you," he informed her, enchanting her again by his imperfect grasp of language. He had a very Chinese way of expressing himself.

At last, however, he was in bed, looking saintly in his blue

pyjamas, and Elizabeth read him the story of *The Two Bad
Mice*, while Julia, a very independent young woman, bathed
herself. She was forced to seek help in unplaiting her hair,
and Elizabeth brushed it for her with long slow strokes.

"Aunt Beth, will you try to make Mummy let me have it
cut?" begged the child, as she sat patiently enduring.

"Why, darling? Don't you like having plaits?" asked Elizabeth.

"Well, I don't mind really, but it's so hot, and p'raps if it
was cut I'd have curls like you," sighed Julia, looking enviously in the mirror at her aunt's short neat locks.

"Well, yes, you might, but Mummy and Daddy haven't
got curly hair, so you might be disappointed and find yours
was straight too," suggested Elizabeth.

"Oh, well, when I'm a big lady I can have a permutation
like Mummy," said Julia hopefully.

Elizabeth looked solemn.

"So you could," she said. "But I expect you'll have it cut
then anyway. I think Mummy likes it long, doesn't she?"

"Yes, she says it makes me stay tidy," grumbled Julia.
"And I can't even do it myself. All the girls at school can do
their own hair, and so could I if it was cut off."

"Well, I'll suggest it to Mummy, and perhaps she'll think
about it again," said Elizabeth.

"If you tell her it will look nicer short, she'll have to let
me," said Julia emphatically. "You're the head of that magazine, *Egliance*, I know, Mummy has it every month, and so
you must know what's best."

"*Elegance*, you mean," corrected Elizabeth with a smile.
"Does she? I didn't know Mummy read it. And I'm not the
head, only a sub-editor."

"Oh, is that all?" said Julia disappointedly, as if she understood, and added, "Yes, Mummy reads it all through, and
then we cut out the pictures of funny ladies in nighties for our
scrap books and Mummy tries out the food on Daddy and he
says, 'My God, what is this muck?'"

"Darling, you mustn't say that, even if Daddy does," re-
proved Elizabeth. She held Julia's long hair back from her

face, curving it against the round smooth cheeks to look as though it was cut short.

"It would suit you," she admitted. "It would make your face look longer."

"Moon-face, I'm called at school," mourned Julia.

"Well, I was called Freckles," said Elizabeth. "That's just as bad."

"You haven't got any freckles now, though," said Julia, looking closely at her aunt's flawless pale skin.

"No, they all went, and so will your moon look," said Elizabeth, kissing the top of the child's head.

"Me want placks," announced Nicholas, suddenly realising what the talk was about and not wishing to be left out.

"Silly, boys don't have plaits," said Julia scornfully. "Really, Nick, you're just too stupid."

"Boys are lucky, they only have a little bit of hair, and it doesn't get in their way and only takes a minute to brush," said Elizabeth, rumpling his soft mop. "Now, come on; tuck up, pets, it's high time you were both asleep. Mummy will be cross if she knows I've let you stay up so late." She hustled Julia into bed and drew the coverings smoothly over them both. Then she kissed them and went to the door. Already they were sleepy after the excitements of the day.

"Goodnight, darlings," she said.

"Can we come and see you in the morning, Aunt Beth?" asked Julia.

"Yes, dear, but not *too* early, wait till seven, please," she begged. She went outside, and was closing the door when Julia said again, "Aunt Beth?"

"What is it, dear?" Elizabeth opened the door again a little way.

"Where is the far away place Uncle Victor's gone to? Is it under the equator."

Elizabeth's hand tightened on the doorknob.

"No, dear, it isn't," she answered quietly.

"When's he coming back again?" The voice was very alert now, in the maddening way typical of children when the adult world is anxious to close them up for the night.

" Not for about three years," said Elizabeth.

"Why not?"

" He's very busy, he's got a lot of work to do," said Elizabeth. " I didn't think you remembered him, Julia."

"Oh, yes, I do a bit; he was so smiley," said the child. "And Mummy has a photo of him stuck in her book. She said I mustn't ever talk about him to Granny and Grandfather. Why's that?"

" Well, he made them very sad, once, a long time ago," said Elizabeth, desperately seeking the right words. " Of course he's sorry now, but Mummy is afraid they would feel unhappy if you talked about him to them."

" Is he in disgrace, then?" demanded Julia.

"Well, yes, he is," admitted Elizabeth.

"But he'll be forgiven when he comes home again?" asked Julia anxiously.

" Oh, yes, of course he will. It will be all right then," said Elizabeth.

" And you'll be able to have lots of babies just like us and live happily ever after," said Julia with satisfaction.

"Yes, so we will," said Elizabeth brightly. " Now you must go to sleep, darling, or you'll be too weary tomorrow to play all those games we've planned."

She went out once more, closing the door firmly behind her, and walked down the passage to her own room, thinking of the extraordinary aptitude of children to remember all the things it would be best if they forgot.

Elizabeth quickly finished unpacking, pausing several times to admire the pretty changes Mrs. Trent had made in the room. That had been a sweet thought, and she was grateful; yet she knew too what it must have meant to her mother-in-law thus to obliterate every last trace of Victor, for this had been his bedroom as a boy.

She brushed out her soft dark hair, and went downstairs to lay the dinner table and put ready the cold meal for when the others came back from the cocktail party. Then she walked slowly down the garden to the brook, and leaned on the little bridge, gazing at the view over the hill. Deliberately she let her thoughts turn towards Richard; for this weekend she would forget both past and future, and live only for the moment. She let herself admit, as she had done at Easter, " I love him."

Then, the weekend had been disappointingly cold, with rainy squalls, but Tuesday had been fine, and after lunch Elizabeth had gone for a walk over the hill. In spite of the weather the weekend had been happy. Striding along over the paths and through the scrub Elizabeth had reflected upon how much she had enjoyed it. As a child may dread the return to school, so now she dreaded the return to London. She thought of her room, empty and bleak in her absence, where no one waited to welcome her. She thought of her office, where she was held in esteem because she worked hard and with intelligence, and knew she would not mind if she never saw it again. She thought of Susan, returning with insincere grumbles to the household chores on which she thrived, and envied the close quartet of that little family. She thought of Hugh, who, though a little pompous, was a kind and comforting husband on whom Susan relied increasingly for friendship and support. She thought of Richard. Then she remembered her own grim, unavoidable future, and was afraid.

Suddenly, no longer able to maintain the staunch courage that upheld her, she had begun to weep. Stumblingly, blindly, she walked along, with the tears streaming down her face. She walked right into Richard's arms as he returned from visiting a cottage on the hill top. He held her tenderly, not speaking, until in a few seconds she regained control.

" How dreadful of me, I'm so sorry, Richard," she said, drawing back a little from him. Inadequately she tried to dry her eyes with her small handkerchief. He produced a large, clean white one from his pocket, and with awkward gentleness offered it to her.

" No one can be brave all the time, Beth," he said. " It will do you good to let go for a bit."

Suddenly conscious of their proximity to one another, they moved apart, and Elizabeth said in a wondering voice, " You called me Beth!"

He looked embarrassed. "It slipped out. I always think of you as Beth; I'm sorry," he said.

"I like it," she answered gravely. "Only my mother and Susan's children have ever called me that."

She pushed the hair back from her forehead, and tried to smile. "Thank you for the handkerchief," she said, giving it back to him.

Richard put it in his pocket and looked at her searchingly.

"What was it that you couldn't bear any longer?" he asked. "Would it help to talk about it"

"I don't know," she said slowly. "Everyone is so frightened of mentioning it; there isn't anyone to talk about it to."

"There's me," he said simply. "I don't mean as a parson, Beth." Consciously he used the name then. "I mean just as a friend, who is—who loves you," he ended with determination. For a moment he looked defiant, uttering at last the words he had never expected to say.

Elizabeth looked at him intently.

"As you love all your parishioners," she stated slowly.

He shook his head. "No," said Richard steadily. "Not a bit like that."

For a moment she did not answer. She stared at him incredulously. Then, "Oh, poor Richard," she said, so softly that he had to bend his head to hear. "But you make me so glad. You see, I was partly crying because of you."

"Beth!" he exclaimed.

"I wouldn't admit it, even to myself, until now," she confessed, looking down at his hand which to her surprise she discovered was firmly holding her own. "But it's such a relief." She laughed, a little nervously, and then said abruptly, "Well, that's that."

"But it isn't," said Richard steadily. "Some people would say we shouldn't have allowed ourselves to feel so deeply, much less admit it, but to love can never be wrong. It's what we do about it that matters. We shall always have this to draw comfort from, whatever the future holds."

She looked at him, and knew with sudden happiness that he was right.

There was a fallen log nearby, and they moved to sit upon it. The air around them was fresh after the rain, and full of summer's promise.

"Your coat will get dirty," said Richard.

"It doesn't matter," she said. They still held hands, both dreading the moment when this interlude would end and they must face life again.

"You make me feel like a boy," said Richard at last.

She smiled then, and her face was radiant.

"I'm so happy, even though it's so awful and I'm miserable too," she confessed. "But it's so hopeless for you, Richard. You must get over it and marry some nice girl—" her voice trailed away.

Richard said, "You sound like Maggie. I don't want to marry some nice girl. This can bring us a lot of happiness, even if we never talk about it again, and even though we can never be like this again." He still held her hand and could not bring himself to release it.

Presently he said, "What are you going to do, Beth?"

She kicked a tussock of grass.

"How much do you know about it?" she asked.

"Only what my predecessor told me—that your husband is in prison and that his name must never be mentioned to the Brigadier."

"The bare bones," she said. "There's so much more to it than that."

"Won't you tell me?" he asked her then.

"Yes, I'd like you to know," she said. She paused for a moment, looking at their joined hands. Then she began to speak.

"Victor and I met in the war," she said. "He was in the R.A.F. He was—is—very good-looking and charming. He was gay, and out for fun, as most people were at that time. We were married just before the war ended. Not very long afterwards he got into trouble; it was to do with the Mess funds. He was President of the Officers' Mess. I had some money that my parents had left me—they were both killed in an air raid—and we were able to square things up, so that he got off. He was very lucky to escape a court martial, but he was due to be demobilised, so they let it drop.

"He was very abject about it, and promised never to do such a thing again. We managed to keep it from his parents, and I was sure he wouldn't be tempted to steal again.

"He got a good job through some connection of his father's, in a big London company. We had a nice flat, and a car, and I suppose life was really quite pleasant. But I began to realise how weak Victor was, and how easy to influence and impress. He was always trying to cut a dash, and wanting me to as well. He kept urging me to buy new clothes, and he was very generous, always giving me extravagant presents. Then one day he came home in awful trouble. He had 'borrowed' some money from the firm, meaning, he said to pay it back later and had been found out.

"Well, they were marvellous—his firm, I mean. I went with him to see them and we paid the money back out of what was left of mine—there wasn't much over by then. Once again he promised never to do such a thing in the future and because of the connection through his father they gave him another chance. I did everything I could think of to make sure he wouldn't—I kept strict accounts of all we spent. But he did do it again. He was gambling, that was where most of it went, though I didn't discover it till he was caught. This time his firm could do nothing but prosecute.

"He got seven years. I don't know how Mrs. Trent survived the trial. It was the most terrible shock, and of course it all had to come out about the other times. Victor's father wouldn't speak to him, once he knew there was no mistake and that he really had done it. He will never forgive him.

"But they did all they could to help. The lawyers' fees were fantastic, that's why the Trents are hard up now, it crippled them to pay them, and the costs; and of course there was all the money he had taken to be paid back too. It ran into thousands.

"I go to see Victor three times a year. He hasn't changed at all; he's just never grown up. He has no sense of responsibility or of right or wrong."

Richard had listened in silence to the sordid little story.

"What you must have gone through, poor Beth," he said slowly.

She smiled sadly. "Well, even before the first occasion I realised he wasn't all that I thought he was," she said. "But I was fond of him, though in the end I despised him for being so weak. But I knew he couldn't altogether help it. If I had been a better and more understanding wife perhaps he would never have done it."

"You can't blame yourself, Beth," said Richard. "You still stuck to him."

"That was my duty," she said gravely. "And he needed me. He still loves me, Richard, that's what's so awful in a way. Now you see why I must go back to him when he comes out."

Richard did not answer.

"If I don't, there's no hope of him keeping straight," she went on. "If I do, there's just a chance that I may be able to keep him on the rails. I'm saving all the money I can, and when he comes out we're going to Canada. He'll get remission of his sentence for good conduct. In Canada he can start all over again. If it doesn't work out after a year or so, perhaps I shall leave him, but I must try to make it a success."

"But what a year you will have, Beth," said Richard in a low voice.

"I dread it. I don't know how I shall bear it," she said frankly. "But I must do it."

"Yes." Richard accepted it. He looked at the slender, fine-boned hand he held, so fragile, it seemed, for so much strength of purpose.

"And if you do leave him, after a year, what then?" he asked.

"I haven't really thought; you see, I mustn't look at it like that. I must do my utmost not to leave him," she said. "If he goes to prison again, or it's completely impossible, then perhaps I would get a separation to be free of him. But of course he would still be my husband."

"Of course," said Richard. "But you really will leave him if it's intolerable?"

"I suppose so, after a fair trial," she said.

"I ought to be telling you to stick to him whatever happens," said Richard bitterly, "but there are limits."

She nodded. "If he won't try to help himself, then I shall have to give it up," she said. "What then? I haven't thought. I can only be so thankful that we never had a child, even though I wanted one so much."

Richard looked at her.

"I hope I never will," she added quietly.

Four months later, leaning on the bridge in the evening light, Elizabeth remembered as clearly as though it had happened yesterday all that they had said. They had not met again until today. Now, though they must never acknowledge their love, it was still between them, an invisible support.

She stirred and looked at her watch. Soon the others would be back from the cocktail party; it was time to return to the house. She looked once more back over the brook to the hill before she moved away. A movement in the bushes at the end of the first field caught her eye, as though a man was walking there. She looked again, but there seemed to be nothing and nobody; it must have been a trick of light.

Elizabeth turned, and walked slowly over the lawn towards the house.

VIII

The cocktail party was hot and noisy, with everyone talking at the top of their voices and some people drinking more than they could comfortably absorb. Mrs. Trent found it hard to understand all that was said to her in the din, for her hearing in crowds was not perfect. Richard, seeing her looking rather bewildered, hemmed into a corner by a stout woman in unsuitable bright yellow silk, took pity on her and crossed the room to rescue her.

After polite exchanges, the yellow silk lady moved away, for the sight of a clerical collar immediately frightened her off, and Richard cleared a path through the crowd to the french window, suggesting it would be pleasant to look at Lady

Faversham's border. One or two other guests strolled along in the mellow light outside, but most of them preferred to cluster together in the heated congestion of the drawing-room.

"Ah, this is better," sighed Mrs. Trent, glad to be out of the smoky atmosphere. "Thank you for rescuing me, Richard. I must also thank you and Mrs. Maggs for finding me a cook, I can't describe to you the difference it will make."

"I'm glad it worked out so conveniently," said Richard with a smile. "Maggie loves running the village, but her schemes don't always bear such rapid fruit."

"She's a wonder, your Maggie," said Mrs. Trent. "What she doesn't know about village gossip hasn't happened, yet she never repeats a word herself."

"She's a marvel. I don't know what I'd do without her," said Richard. "She spoils me dreadfully."

"Well, she won't last for ever," pointed out Mrs. Trent. "You ought to get married, Richard. Then you could spare her when she has to retire."

"I don't think I'm the marrying sort," said Richard lightly.

Mrs. Trent looked at him sharply. "Even if Elizabeth did divorce him, it wouldn't help, would it?" she asked.

Richard was taken aback. Mrs. Trent looked at his startled face, and said more gently, "It's all right, Richard, I only guessed. I wasn't even certain until I saw your face just now. Does she know?"

He nodded.

"Oh, I'm glad. It will comfort her, the poor child," said Mrs. Trent. "But you, Richard. What a dreadful pity it is. You would have made her very happy."

"Well, there it is," said Richard. "As you say, a divorce doesn't help at all. And Elizabeth feels that she must go back to Victor."

"I know," Mrs. Trent sighed. "I have tried to persuade her not to, but it made no difference. I shall try again, before he comes out. Although he's my son, I would rather see him back in prison for the rest of his life than wrecking her existence any longer."

"You won't get her to change her mind," said Richard gently.

"I'm afraid not. That's what I said to Susan today; people like Elizabeth don't change. And of course, she's the only one who has the least influence over Victor. If he won't mend his ways for her, then no one will be able to make him," said Mrs. Trent. "But I feel so dreadful about what it's done to her."

"Of course you do," said Richard. "But it isn't your fault. I imagine he's gone like this as a result of the war."

She shook her head. "No." When he was a child he used to pick up any coins left lying about. He had no sense of property. Once he stole some money from one of the maids. My husband never knew about it. I was so glad when he married Elizabeth; she was just the sort of girl to make him pull himself together. But I ought to have warned her; I shouldn't have let her go into it blindly, and I can never forgive myself for that."

Richard said, "She has great strength. She may triumph yet."

"He still adores her, so perhaps he will manage to keep straight this time," sighed Mrs. Trent. "But I'm very glad she has the comfort of your friendship, Richard. Don't worry, your secret is safe." She smiled then, and suddenly he realised how much she had aged since he first came to Bramsbourne. Her face and neck were very thin, and there were tiny lines around her eyes and on her forehead. Her soft, shining hair was quite white. Though she could not be more than sixty she looked at least seventy years old.

At this moment Susan came striding over the grass towards them. "Ah, there you are, Mummy. I wondered wherever you'd got to," she cried. She held in her hand a half nibbled lobster patty. "Have you had any of these? They're delicious. I've eaten so many I shan't want any supper. Hullo, Richard, how's the church these days? Packed to the doors every Sunday?"

Richard laughed. Susan's bubbling good spirits, like those of her son, were infectious.

"I hope we shall have the pleasure of seeing you there to-morrow to swell the throng," he replied. "How are the children?"

She launched into a recital of their latest exploits, and gradually they returned to the house.

In the hall, frowned over by some lowering antlers, Brigadier Trent was having an earnest discussion with his host about the folly of prisons without bars. It was a subject upon which he felt strongly, and he would sometimes disconcert his friends, whose consideration for his feelings led them to avoid at all costs discussions of so delicate a nature, by suddenly demanding their views, or emphatically stating his own. It was as though he got a curious satisfaction from grasping such a nettle so firmly.

"What's the good of sending boys to prison or Borstal if you don't make it damned uncomfortable for them while they're there, eh?" he now demanded fiercely, raising his bushy white eyebrows. "Stands to reason, if it's as pleasant as they make it nowadays the lads won't mind going back there again. Besides, look at what it costs us taxpayers, keeping 'em in luxury. It's a scandal, that's what it is. You should bring it up in the Lords, Charlie."

Lord Faversham replied with calm, "Doubt if I'd be able to achieve much, my dear fellow. Too much red tape about nowadays."

The two men were old friends and understood one another perfectly. Lord Faversham was perhaps the only person who fully understood his companion's curious preoccupation with prison reform. By such conversations he could still show courage, although he was too much shattered to talk about his son.

"I see in tonight's paper two chaps have escaped from Moorhurst Jail," added Lord Faversham, not changing the subject as so many of his friends would have done in their embarrassment.

The Brigadier snorted. "Hmph, silly fools. Sure to be caught, sure to be caught," he said, and then, "Where have those women got to? Never can get them home in decent time for dinner. Good party, Charlie; thank you. Not in my line to stay too long. See you on Monday for luncheon, eh?"

" We're looking forward to it," said his host.

" You'll have that film star feller with you, eh? Damn lot of nonsense," said the Brigadier.

" Oh, yes, he'll be coming along. You'll like him, Jack. He's not a bad chap at all," said Lord Faversham.

Another snort was the Brigadier's only reply to this statement.

As they drove homewards along the winding country road they passed a police car going slowly in the opposite direction. Faintly they could hear the hum of its wireless operating.

" I wonder what they're doing, prowling around on a Saturday night," said Susan.

"Faversham said two idiots had escaped from Moorhurst," grunted her father. " Probably they're looking for them."

Sitting in the back, beside Mrs. Trent, Susan involuntarily glanced at her mother. The eyes of the two women met briefly, apprehensively.

Under cover of the confusion getting out of the car when they arrived back at the Priory, Susan whispered, " It wouldn't be him, Mummy, he'd have more sense."

" Of course," said Mrs. Trent tersely. Then, " Don't mention this to Elizabeth, Susan."

" No, it would only upset her," agreed the younger woman. " Don't worry, Mummy. It was just a coincidence that it was Moorhurst."

IX

Susan and Elizabeth washed up the dinner things while Hugh and his parents-in-law talked over coffee in the drawing-room. As she had promised, Elizabeth put in a plea for Julia's hair to be cut, and Susan agreed to think about it again. They talked for a while, lightly, as they dealt swiftly with the pile of plates and glasses.

" It's fantastic how many good woman-hours one wastes doing this," said Susan. " I wish mother would get a machine."

"It would be worth it when we're all here," said Elizabeth. "I know someone who's got one. It's marvellous, you just put everything inside it and switch it on, and they all come out clean and dry."

"Wonderful," said Susan. "Whatever do they cost? I shall buy one when I win the pools."

Elizabeth laughed. "I can't think how you understand them," she said, "I can't make head or tail of the forms."

"Neither can I really," said Susan. "But you don't have to, you just put down a lot of noughts. I put the children's birth-days, and ours, and Rusty's, and so on. One day they'll turn up, you'll see. Then I'll take you on the spree, Elizabeth."

"What fun," said Elizabeth. "You'd better teach me how to do them too, Sue, and then we'll have a double chance of suc-cess."

"Yes, we might form a syndicate," said Susan ambitiously. Presently she said more seriously, "Elizabeth, you said you wouldn't mind talking about it; are you quite determined to go back to Victor when he comes out?"

Her sister-in-law nodded. "Yes, quite," she said.

"I do wish you wouldn't," said Susan. "It won't be any good, you know."

"Well, I must give it a try," said Elizabeth.

Susan vigorously rubbed the glass she was drying. "I wish you'd think of yourself over this. What sort of a life have you got? If you divorced him, you could marry again, and have a proper life, as you ought."

Elizabeth answered gently, "But, Susan, even if I did divorce him, that doesn't unmarry us. I wouldn't feel free to marry again."

"I can't understand that," said Susan, furrowing her brow as she tried. "Why should you be lonely always just because of some old-fashioned idea of the Church's?"

Elizabeth said, "I know it's an out-of-date view, but Victor and I were married for better or worse, for life. Just because it's for worse, in some respects, doesn't mean one can abandon it."

Susan sighed. "It's such a dreadful waste. It's a pity he wasn't locked up for life," she said.

"Don't say that, Sue," said Elizabeth. "There's a lot that's good in Victor, as you know. He's gay and generous, too generous, that's partly the trouble. I have every hope that he'll pull himself together when he comes out. It isn't much fun in gaol, you know."

"I don't expect it is," said Susan. "How is he? Mummy longs to go and see him, but she thinks she wouldn't be able to bear it. Father doesn't even want to know where he is."

"He's quite well. Thinner, you know, and he doesn't talk much. I tell him about Canada, and all the openings there are there, trying to give him something to look forward to. He's desperately sorry for the unhappiness he's caused,," Elizabeth told her. "He longs for your mother's letters, but he won't risk writing to her in case your father discovered, he's terrified of him."

"I know. That's partly the cause of all this, if you ask me," said Susan. "When we were small, father was incredibly strict, especially with Victor, because he was a boy. He expected far more from him than he was capable of—Victor wasn't a superman, like father had been. He was rather a coward about climbing trees and so on, and not very brainy, and father couldn't bear to have a son who didn't measure up to his own high standards. That's why mummy took to shielding him when he'd been naughty, coping with him herself. It was the greatest pity, because when he did really bad things, like stealing from the maids, a good beating from father would probably have cured him once and for all."

"Did he really do that as a child?" asked Elizabeth.

"Oh, yes, didn't you know?" Susan was surprised.

"No, I didn't," said Elizabeth slowly. She laid a vegetable dish face downwards on the draining board and fished in the sink for its lid, thinking with curious relief that she was not the original cause of his extravagance.

"I thought mummy told you, when it all blew up," said Susan. "But perhaps she thought there wasn't much point."

"Poor Victor," said Elizabeth. "He isn't altogether to blame."

"Well, I think he is," said Susan stoutly. "If he'd had a

bit more character he wouldn't have done it, however badly he needed the money. We don't all go about pinching things just because we're hard up."

"No, of course not," Elizabeth had to smile at Susan's vehemence. "But most of us have some sense of right and wrong which stops us, and I don't think Victor has. He's never said he was sorry for what he's done, only for the misery he caused."

"Well, it's high time he did grow a conscience," said Susan. "And anyway, we're getting right away from the point of this discussion, which was, must you go with him to Canada?"

"Yes, I must," said Elizabeth firmly. "It's sweet of you to be concerned for me, but I should feel guilty all my life if I didn't have one more try."

"Well, if I can ever help at all, send the money for you to come back or anything, for Victor won't have it, I will some-how; you let me know," said Susan gruffly.

"Bless you, Sue, I won't forget," said Elizabeth gratefully.

"I still think you're off your head," said Susan frankly. She picked up the tray of gleaming glasses to carry them back to the pantry. As she walked out of the kitchen a dark shape rose from the floor, unseen beneath her load by Susan. There was a yelp, then a tremendous clatter and crash as she stumbled over Rusty, patiently waiting for her outside the door, and her mother's best glasses lay in fragments on the floor.

"Gosh, that's done it," said Susan, torn between dismay and a desire to laugh.

"Have you cut yourself?" asked Elizabeth, appearing with a dustpan and brush.

"No, but what will mummy say? All her glasses smashed to smithereens, and umpteen people coming to lunch on Mon-day! And all the shops shut!" Susan looked as much abashed as in her clumsier schooldays.

"Never mind, I expect we can borrow some," said Elizabeth soothingly. "Poor old Rusty, did it give you a fright?" she patted the dog, unwitting cause of the disaster, who watched them with large, pathetic eyes. "The Favershams will lend us some. I must say, Sue, you fielded that tray very neatly." She held aloft two sherry glasses that had escaped undamaged, and began to laugh.

"You really did look rather funny," she explained.

Susan sighed. " I biffed my elbow," she complained, rubbing it. "Oh, well, worse things happen at sea, I suppose," she added philosophically, and she too began to laugh; then, bending down, chuckling, the two young women started to clear up the wreckage.

X

The last bus did not penetrate down the winding lane to Bramsbourne, but stopped on the main road and forced its passengers to walk the rest of the way. Ivy and Alan, descending from it, took the field path back to the village. She was still in a drugged trance from her session at the cinema, and disposed to be kind to the young man. Hand in hand, they walked along through the scented meadows. As they skirted the field that bordered the Priory garden they could hear the brook flowing past; it was dusk, and the air was still. Daringly Alan released Ivy's hand and put his arm around her; still more daringly he halted, bent forward and clumsily kissed her cheek.

"Why, Alan Blake !" exclaimed Ivy, surprised and a little shaken, yet not at all displeased. She felt soft and warm in his arms; she exuded a fragrance of "Wild Desire " perfume; above all, she had neither immediately hit him, nor pushed him away. Dizzy with success, Alan took a deep breath, and disregarding their heavy coating of lipstick, awkwardly sought her lips.

Ivy was a healthy young woman, and subconsciously this was just what she needed. For a moment she wondered whether to make a scene, but before she could decide, she was responding to his young, inexpert kisses. If she closed her eyes, she could almost imagine it was Harley Darrell embracing her, though it was true that Alan lacked some of his finesse. She opened her eyes for a better comparison, and a sudden movement beyond Alan's left ear attracted her attention.

"Why, whoever's that," she cried, abruptly breaking free. "Alan, behave yourself. There's someone watching us over by that haystack."

Alan looked perfunctorily round.

"There's no one there, Ivy," he said, still in a daze.

"But there is, I distinctly saw a man move along the hedge," she insisted. "Well, whoever it is, I'm not waiting here for him to watch me. Come along, Alan, and for goodness sake wipe your face, you do look a sight."

Deflated, the young man sheepishly wiped her lipstick from his mouth with his handkerchief, and followed her indignant back down the path. But he was not discouraged, for he felt that tonight he had successfully accomplished a major operation.

He left her at the door of the Rose and Crown. The last customers had gone and her father was closing up for the night.

"Are you coming round tomorrow?" Ivy asked, standing, hand on hip in the doorway.

"'Fraid not, I'm on duty," he said unhappily.

"Well, I'm sure I don't mind," said Ivy haughtily, "I'm not at all interested."

"Ivy, you know I'd come if I could," he said urgently. The memory of her soft, albeit sticky, lips pricked him on to add, against his better judgment, "Will you think over what I said today, about us? I mean, about us getting married?"

Ivy laughed in his face.

"Think it over, indeed," she jeered. "When I get married, it will be to somebody who can really get things done, a real he-man, not a tuppeny-ha'penny chap like you." She turned on her heel and went into the inn, banging the door behind her.

Left alone outside, Alan stood for a moment dejectedly looking at the closed door. Then he turned and fetched his bicycle from the shed, to begin his long ride back to the aerodrome.

Within the Rose and Crown, Bert Higgs scolded his daughter.

"That's a fine way to treat a young man, my girl," he said, "Banging the door on him like that, when he's given you a nice day out. Why didn't you ask him in?"

"I've had enough of him, that's why, the soppy thing," said Ivy crossly.

"And I should think he's had enough of you, too," said her father, eyeing her with distaste. "Look at you, lipstick all over your face, and what you've been sitting in I don't know."

Ivy twisted round to look at the back of her skirt. The white piqué that had been so fresh this afternoon was smeared and stained, grey and green, from her rustic hour in the none too clean punt.

"My dress," she wailed, "Oh, whatever shall I do?" and she ran out of the room. Her father watched her go, and shook his head sadly. "I ought to have taken the slipper to you years ago, my girl," he thought unhappily.

Upstairs Ivy stormed about her bedroom. She was furious with Alan for being the unwitting cause of the damage to her expensive dress, regardless of the fact that it was hardly suitable for an afternoon such as they had spent. Angrily she wondered how many people whom she knew had seen her walking through the town with a grimy rear to her skirt, tittering about it and saving it up to describe to their friends later, so that they might all tease her. She was enraged too at her own weakness in yielding to Alan's kisses, and certain that the unknown watcher whom she had seen in the field would report it round the village and make her again a laughing-stock.

"Marry him, indeed," she fumed, savagely wiping the powder and paint off her face. "Not if he was the last man in the world, I wouldn't."

She creamed her cheeks fiercely with "Moonbalm" and jumped into bed. There, in the sheltering darkness, with no one to watch her struttings and posturings, Ivy Higgs experienced a strange sensation. She saw again the tender, anxious look in Alan's grey eyes, and remembered the comfortable feeling of his strong young arms, and two slow, large tears crept out between her lashes and ran down her face.

XI

It had been a long day, and Elizabeth was not sorry when at last it was time for bed. She dawdled about upstairs, enjoying the soothing luxury of a bath with water that was really hot, and pottering round in her pretty bedroom, brushing her hair and filing her nails. There was nothing left in this room now to remind her again of Victor; and when she thought about him, overwhelming pity for her mother-in-law filled Elizabeth. However, her talks with Susan and with Julia were enough reminders of the past for the time being, and she was determined to enjoy this weekend to the full without thinking about the future.

She got into bed, and read for a little while, but her attention wandered from the book and she found herself back in the churchyard talking with Richard, watching his eyes crinkle at the corners when he smiled, and the way his hair grew thickly back from his forehead. He won't go bald with such a mop, she thought in fond foolishness, but she had seen today a few grey hairs above his ears. She would not brood about the loneliness they both must feel; tonight she would only think of happy things.

Presently she fell asleep.

It was after midnight when a scraping sound disturbed her. Elizabeth started into wakefulness. Something was scrabbling about outside her window. She lay still and tense, with her heart pounding, hearing the noise get louder and closer, until at last she saw the figure of a man appear silhouetted against the sky in the window-frame.

Wild plans of screaming or of feigning sleep crossed her mind. There was nothing worth stealing in this room; perhaps, when he had discovered that, the burglar would move on in search of better fortune, and she would be able to creep up behind him and hit him on the head, she thought valorously. She had been holding her breath with fright as he climbed into the room, but now she could hold it no longer and without thinking released it in a sigh.

"Are you awake? Don't be frightened, Elizabeth," whispered the intruder.

She sat up at once, in instant, horrified recognition.

"Victor!" she gasped. "What are you doing here? Where have you come from? What's happened?"

He came towards her and sat down on the bed.

"I guessed you'd have this room," he said. "I'm on the run, I got out last night. I had to see you again before I hopped it."

"You've escaped?" She looked at him, appalled, in the darkness. "You must be mad, Victor," she exclaimed.

He stretched out a hand and switched on the bedside light. She saw that he was very dirty, but smiling in the old, self-satisfied way she had come to dread.

"I fixed it months ago," he said proudly. "A chap who came out two weeks back helped me to get clear, once I'd broken out, and found these clothes for me. There was another fellow with me, but we thought we'd stand a better chance if we separated. I'm on my way to Hull, to jump a cargo boat. Another pal of mine has promised to try and smuggle me on board if I can get there in time."

"But Victor, you haven't a chance! You're bound to be caught, you'll never get away," she cried. "Why, every policeman in the country will be looking for you. Whatever made you do it? They'll catch you and you'll lose your good conduct remission. Oh, you shouldn't have done it."

"But they're not going to find me," said Victor confidently. "Only I must have some money, Elizabeth, that's where you can help me. You must get me some. I can't get out of the country unless I have plenty of money."

She was stunned, watching him in utter dismay.

"Victor, you must give yourself up," she insisted. "Perhaps if you do that, they won't be too hard on you. I'll drive you in to the police station." She made as if to get out of bed, but he stopped her.

"I won't give myself up," he said quietly, looking at her. How lovely she was, with her eyes wide in fright and surprise, and her dark hair unruly.

"Have you thought what this will do to your parents?" she demanded. "You've given them enough unhappiness without this. Your escape will be in every paper and there'll be another dreadful scandal."

"If I can get right away, to South America, as I plan, they'll never have to worry about me again," said Victor. "Only I must have money, Elizabeth."

"But we were going to Canada; you agreed; you were going to go straight," she said wildly, her usual calm entirely gone.

"I hadn't forgotten, but I couldn't let you do that," he said with unusual gentleness. "I'll always remember what you were willing to do, Elizabeth, and be grateful, but I've dragged you down enough. I've seen you searching for things to talk about when you came to see me at Moorhurst. I knew what an impossible ordeal it would be for you. I knew you'd made up your mind to it, so I didn't argue, but I love you, though you may think I have a poor way of showing it, and I don't want to bring you any more unhappiness. That's why I must succeed in this escape. South America is the best place to aim for, they don't ask so many questions there, and there are plenty of openings if you can make a few contacts." He did not say what sort of openings he meant. "I'll write to you when I'm safe, and you can get a divorce and be rid of me."

"But I don't want a divorce, I want us to try again. I'm sure everything will be all right," she protested.

"No, Elizabeth," he said. "I've been weak before, but this time I know what I'm going to do. I will try and keep straight, really I will, but I must do it alone. The less you have to do with me the better." There was a new firmness about his mouth as he spoke.

Elizabeth looked at him with misgiving. Then, in a small voice, she said, "You're not to see your mother, you've done enough to her. You mustn't see any of the others."

"I won't," he said, relaxing a little as he realised that she was beginning to yield. "I wouldn't have come here only that I did want to see you again, Elizabeth, and I had to get some money somehow."

"I haven't got much," she said, reaching for her handbag which lay on the table beside her. She took out her wallet, a slim, expensive leather one with her initial that Victor had given her six years ago.

"There's only five pounds," she said, counting it out, "will that be enough?"

"Nowhere near," he said, with a ghost of his old gay laugh. "What shall we do? Go and rob the others while they're asleep?"

"Don't be an idiot," she said angrily, in no mood for jokes. "That would only raise a burglar scare in the morning. I could borrow some from Sue, and perhaps from your mother, tomorrow. They're sure to have some. How much do you want, Victor?"

"At least fifty quid," he said. "The whole thing will fail if I can bribe my way through."

"Yes, I see," she said slowly. "But you ought to move on, you shouldn't hang about here. They'll be searching for you; surely this is the first place where they'll look," she said, and knew as she spoke that she was committed to helping him.

"I'll keep off the roads," said Victor, "I've been promised a lift on Monday night with the roundabout that's coming for the Flower Show. They're going north after they've come here. Funny how that old Flower Show still goes on."

"It's quite warm tonight. You could hide up in the fields," she said, thinking aloud, "but anyone could find you, a child, or a dog."

"What about the cellar?" he suggested. "It's summer, so they won't be using the heating boiler. No one ever used to go down there in the summer."

"Yes, I suppose that would be fairly safe," said Elizabeth. "But Julia and Nick might go there, playing hide and seek or something."

"We could lock it, they'd think the key had got lost," he said.

"But supposing the police come here looking for you? They'd be sure to search the whole house," said Elizabeth, trying to think of every possibility.

"I could hide under the coke. I'm dirty enough as it is," he said with his old grin that had once been irresistible to Elizabeth.

"You must have some food," she said, becoming practical. She got out of bed and put on her dressing-gown. "Come on, we'd better get it all fixed while everyone's asleep."

Victor stood up and watched her. He was dirty and dishevelled, with his short hair on end. "Let me look at you for a moment, Elizabeth," he begged, "just so that I can remember you. Don't be afraid, I won't touch you."

She felt a stab of pity for him. "Poor Victor, you haven't a chance of getting away, but I hope you do," she whispered, and she gently kissed him. "Good luck," she said.

Then she quietly opened the door and peered out. "Susan's used to sleeping with one ear open in case the children wake, we must be very careful or she may hear us," she explained. "We'll go down the back stairs."

They crept cautiously along the passage and round the corner to the winding flight of stairs that led down into the scullery. There was no sound. Rusty, sleeping in Susan's room, was busy dreaming of rabbits and did not hear them. Outside the house a flight of stone steps led down into the cellar, which was large and shaped like an L, with little odd corners and crannies, in one of which stood the big old boiler that in winter fed the central heating. Elizabeth had found a torch on the way, and in its light they saw the spectral mounds of coke, silently waiting for the winter. The atmosphere was damp and dusty.

"Ugh, how horrid," said Elizabeth. A mouse pattered over the stone flagged floor and vanished with a scamper. "You won't be very comfortable."

"That's nothing new," he said ruefully.

She found the big key hanging on a nail near the door. "You'd better keep this," she said. "And only unlock the door if you're sure it's me. I'll knock three times. Now I'll go and get you some food and a rug. I'll bring you as much money as I can collect tomorrow night, after everyone's asleep; it won't be safe to come here during the day in case anyone sees. Then on Monday you can move on, without waiting for the round-about. You'll be far less likely to be noticed if you travel with the holiday crowds. I'll bring some things so that you can have a shave first," she added, with a glance at his bristly chin.

She left him then, and went quickly back into the house. In the hall chest she found an old rug, a bit the worse for moth, and took it down to him. Then she went to the kitchen and made coffee, which she poured into a thermos flask, hoping nobody would take it into their heads to go for a picnic tomorrow. Recklessly she took the legs off the two cold chickens left over from lunch which were in the larder, and cut some slices of bread and butter. All the time she was in a feverish hurry in case someone heard her and came to investigate.

She left Victor at last, locked into his new prison, sitting on the rug which he had spread over a mound of coke, gnawing at a chicken leg. Then she went back to bed.

It was two o'clock in the morning.

PART THREE

SUNDAY

I

The morning air was fresh and sweet as Richard walked to the church to prepare for his eight o'clock service. He opened the main door in readiness for the congregation when they arrived before he went into the vestry. As he entered the dark little room a figure moved forward from the shadows in the corner. Richard looked in surprise at the thin young man who stood before him.

"Good morning," he said. "What can I do for you?"

"You're the vicar?" the man asked suspiciously. Richard saw that his clothes were dirty and unkempt and he was none too clean himself.

"Yes," he said. "Are you in trouble? What's the matter?"

"I'm Victor Trent," said the visitor, and seeing the expression on Richard's face he went on quickly, "I see my name means something to you. I want some money."

Richard stared. He said, "You've broken out of gaol! Are you mad? You must give yourself up at once."

"Not on your sweet life," said the young man. "I'm out, and I'm staying out, and you won't spill the beans either. I can claim sanctuary here in the church."

"But you can't stay here; you'll be found when you leave," said Richard. He thought rapidly, trying to decide the best course of action.

"I'll leave when you've given me some money," said Victor grimly.

"If you think I'm going to help you to escape from the police you're mistaken," Richard told him firmly.

"You will," said Victor confidently. He rocked to and fro on his heels with his hands in his pockets, watching, while Richard looked at him in dismay. So this was Elizabeth's husband!

"I saw you yesterday afternoon, coming out of this church with my wife," said Victor now. "Nice goings on for a parson, I must say. How'd you like me to split? Oh, I can find a way to tell, even if I am on the run, and unless you find me twenty pounds by evening I'll do it. Even if you don't mind everyone knowing, Elizabeth will," he finished.

Richard took no notice. He glanced at his watch. "I've got a service in ten minutes," he said. "You must clear out during it. There will be people going in and out of church all day, you can't possibly stay here."

"I'll go if you'll bring the money tonight," said Victor. "And I don't think you'll tell the police, Mr. Richard Dell, because that would make a lot of trouble for my wife, and you wouldn't like that, would you?" He smiled then, but without any trace of the charm he had displayed to Elizabeth. He did not really mean his blackmailing words, but he could never resist any opportunity to threaten or struggle for power.

"You must keep away from Elizabeth," said Richard sternly. "She mustn't know you're here."

Victor saw no point in telling Richard that he had already spoken to his wife. "I'll keep away from her, and disappear in the night, if you bring the cash," he said. "Twenty pounds, mind—more if possible, but I know the banks are shut." He moved back a pace. "There's a loose stone by the water butt outside. Put it under there, and then I can collect it when it suits me," he said, and retreated back into the shadows. "I'll be gone when the service is over," he added.

"God help you," said Richard quietly. There was no time for further talk. He hurried back into the church to light the candles and finish his preparations, with no chance to think about the fantastic situation before his service began. When it had ended, Victor had vanished.

Maggie was busy getting his breakfast ready when he arrived back at the Vicarage, and a tantalising smell of bacon and egg greeted him. There was nothing to be gained by delaying and upsetting Mrs. Maggs, so Richard ate quickly, thinking hard. He could not decide what to do. Obviously he should telephone to the police immediately, but if they caught Victor close to his home the news was bound to get out, and it would be so distressing for Elizabeth and the Trents. If he was not captured until he had moved into another district it might not upset them so much. He did not consider Victor's attempt at blackmail, for he recognised it as an empty threat. Oh, you foolish young man, thought Richard, trying such bravado when you have a loyal wife waiting to help you at the end of your sentence. The main thing was to hope she need never know that he had been back to the village. Richard got up from the dining-table and went to see how much money there was in the house. He found fifteen pounds, some in his wallet and some church funds waiting to be banked. Then he called from the hall, " Maggie dear, can you lend me any money?"

" Why, whatever for, Master Dick?" she cried. " You can't want any money on Sunday, except what you put in the collection."

" I can't explain now, but I must have some. Be a dear, Maggie. You shall have it back as soon as I can get to the bank."

" Well, I don't know, I'm sure," grumbled Maggie, going off muttering to herself. She came back a few minutes later with five pound notes. " There you are, Richard, but I'm sure I don't know what's got into you," she complained.

Richard gave her a hug. " You're a dear, Maggie. I'm very sorry about it, and I'll explain later," he said.

" Well, I don't know," repeated Mrs. Maggs to herself, still bewildered. She went back to her kitchen and Richard moved to his desk, where he sealed the money in a stout envelope.

The telephone bell interrupted his anxious thoughts; he lifted the receiver and a worried voice said at once, " Oh, Richard, is that you?"

He recognised Elizabeth. " Yes, what is it, Beth?" he asked quickly.

"Oh, Richard, I'm sorry to bother you so early, and on a Sunday when you're so busy, but could you possibly lend me some money? I've been so stupid and come away without any."

"Elizabeth dear, of course I can," he said, thinking rapidly. What an extraordinary coincidence! Had that scoundrel somehow contacted her after all? Surely she would say if that had happened, but perhaps she was afraid of being overheard. Anyway, whatever she wanted it for, she must have the money. "It's no bother," he went on. "How much do you want?"

"Can you spare ten pounds?" she asked. Her voice was calmer now.

"Yes, certainly. When would you like it? Shall I give it to you after church?"

"Oh, Richard, thank you. I'm terribly grateful. I'm so sorry to have to ask you," she said.

"That's all right, I'm glad you did," he replied. "Elizabeth, is everything all right? You'd tell me if there was anything wrong? You sound upset."

"I'm not, really Richard. I expect I'm tired, I didn't sleep very well," she answered, and laughed a little breathlessly. "Here comes Julia, I must fly. A thousand thanks."

She rang off, and he replaced his receiver slowly. Something unusual must be happening at the Priory, he was convinced. Elizabeth was seldom ruffled from her normal calm, and it was fantastic that she should need so large a sum as ten pounds on a Sunday morning. The suspicion that she knew of Victor's whereabouts grew stronger in his mind as he slit the envelope he had just closed and took out ten pounds. Then he looked at his watch; there was just time to go down to the Rose and Crown and ask Bert Higgs to cash a cheque before matins.

II

Ivy Higgs woke up with a splitting headache and a guilty conscience. She dragged herself downstairs to cook the breakfast, first splashing her face in cold water at the sink. Her father looked at her frosty expression and decided that silence was his best attitude today; accordingly he disappeared behind the newspaper while he drank tea and demolished a large plate of sausage and bacon.

The hot strong tea revived Ivy, and her natural egoism began to triumph over her morning depression. Thinks he can marry me, indeed, she thought scornfully, clattering the dishes into the sink, who does he think he is, I should like to know. I'll show him, I'll show everyone, just let them wait and see. She began to wash up very noisily.

Her father gave a snort as an item in the paper caught his eye.

"Hm, seen this, Ive?" he dared to remark.

"Seeing as how you've had the paper solid since it arrived, how could I?" she demanded pertly. Then, for she was always inquisitive, "What is it?"

"'Two convicts escape,'" he read, "'Early yesterday morning two prisoners escaped from Moorhurst Gaol. The men, who got out by a daring climb over a twenty-foot wall topped with iron spikes and jagged glass, are believed to have separated after leaving the vicinity of the prison. Their prison uniforms were found by police in a deserted alley, and it is thought that outside contacts helped them to get away. Details and a description of the men in our later editions.' Hm. Wonder what they've done," said Mr. Higgs. He was a student of crime and spent hours poring over the cases in the Sunday papers.

"Moorhurst. That's where young Trent is, isn't it?" asked Ivy, roused to interest by this piece of news.

"Believe it is," said her father, puffing at his pipe. "But he wouldn't be one of 'em. More likely to be a murderer that's got out," he added hopefully. "And don't you go talking about young Trent either, my girl. We don't want to remind anyone about that business."

"Oh, all right Dad," said Ivy crossly. "Can't a person even think?" She set a cup down upon the draining board with such violence that it broke.

"There, now see what you've done. More haste less speed," said her father. Ivy was about to make a sharp retort when there was a knock at the door.

"Go and see who it is, there's a good girl," said Mr. Higgs.

Ivy went grumblingly off, wiping her hands on her apron. When she came back she was followed by Richard.

"It's Mr. Dell, Dad," she announced, angry at being caught by Richard, whom secretly she greatly admired, without her armour of make-up.

"'Morning, Bert," said Richard. "Sorry to disturb you like this."

"Oh, that's all right, sir. Always pleased to see you," said the innkeeper, rising to his feet. "'Fraid you've caught us not quite ship-shape, though." He liked to use nautical expressions when talking to one who had been in the Navy.

"Well, I'm very early," Richard said apologetically. "I expect you take things a bit more quietly on Sunday, eh, Bert?" he added with a smile.

"Have a cup of tea," suggested Bert. "Fetch another cup for the vicar, Ivy," he called.

"Thank you, Ivy," said Richard, with the smile that reminded that foolish girl of Harley Darrell at his most tender. "How nice you look this morning."

She blushed, and the warm colour flooding her face gave her an increased look of beauty. She began to mutter, but Richard went on talking. "You're such a pretty girl, Ivy, it's a pity you don't always leave your face alone. You look much nicer like this without all that stuff on."

Ivy looked from Richard to her father, and began to frown.

"You're all against me," she said furiously, "don't want me to look my best, you don't, none of you. I'll show you," she cried, and dashed out of the room. The two men exchanged meaning glances as they heard her feet pounding up the stairs flying to seek the solace of her powder-pot.

Bert sighed expressively. "There you are, sir, that's what I get," he said. "Wants a good spanking, she does."

Richard entirely agreed with this statement, but felt that

perhaps Ivy was now too old to receive what she deserved in that direction.

" I think she had a row with young Alan last night, too," went on her unhappy father. " She hasn't spoken a civil word since."

"Oh, dear," said Richard. " Bert, why don't you think about letting her get a job away from home? If she went into Haverstoke every day and mixed with other girls she might lose these ideas, although I know you've got plenty for her to do here. The independence might do her good."

" Perhaps it would," said Bert reflectively. " She might start to realise that other girls aren't so silly."

" Well, I think a lot of them are, when they first grow up, till they get some more sense," said Richard.

" Film stars, that's all she thinks about," sighed Mr. Higgs. " And now there's that Harley Darrell coming here tomorrow; we shall never hear the end of it. Girls! Whatever do they think they're up to, I'd like to know?"

Richard felt that his perplexity was justified, and his own remarks had done nothing to relieve the situation.

" Well, you think about it, and I'll talk to her again, when she's in a better mood," he suggested. " I made a mistake in bringing the subject up today, if she's had a quarrel with her young man. I really came round to ask you if you could cash a cheque for me Bert."

Mr. Higgs was one of those rare people who do not expect a detailed explanation for every action.

" Of course, sir," he said at once. " I'll be pleased to." He got to his feet and went to fetch the big tin money box where he kept his takings. " How much do you want?"

III

After breakfast Elizabeth and Susan made the beds together, and while they were thus employed, Elizabeth said, " Sue, could you possibly lend me some money? I'm awfully sorry, I've come away without any, so silly of me."

" Well, I've got two or three pounds you can have, of

course," said Susan, her round face puzzled, "but whatever do you want money for on Sunday? Or is it half a crown for the collection you want?"

"Well, no, it was some pounds, really," said Elizabeth. "I know it sounds odd, Sue, but I can't explain. I'll tell you about it another time. I'll give you a cheque."

"Oh, that's all right, silly," said Susan, "but it does seem queer, wanting all that on a Sunday."

"Yes I know," said Elizabeth, without trying to explain any further.

"Most peculiar," continued Susan. She looked curiously at Elizabeth, who remained silent, and then fetched her handbag. There were four pounds inside it. "Will that do?" she asked.

"Oh, that's marvellous, thank you so much, Sue," said Elizabeth gratefully. That made nineteen with her own five and Richard's promised ten; she had not liked to ask him for more. She wondered how to get hold of the rest of the sum she needed, and thought hard. Mrs. Trent would think her request just as strange as Susan had done, and so would Hugh and Brigadier Trent. Perhaps the Post Office would cash a cheque for her.

No one had complained of hearing mysterious noises in the night, so Victor's installation in the cellar had not been detected. Elizabeth tried to be calm, but she could not stop thinking of him hiding down there, feeling afraid and wondering how near the police were. She prayed that he would get away without discovery. She had not slept until it was almost day, and then when Julia and Nick had come to wake her she was so deeply asleep that she could scarcely rouse herself. As a result, she now had a headache and felt tense and frightened. With all the police in England looking for him, how could Victor escape?

Everyone agreed that Nicholas was too young to go to church. He could not be expected to sit quietly and behave, so he was allowed to stay at home, thereby also giving Susan an excuse for an idle morning. Accordingly everyone else set off down the road at twenty to eleven wearing their tidiest clothes. Julia skipped along in her short blue frock with her pigtails flapping and her school hat on the back of her head. Hugh and the Brigadier, who never ran short of conversation, walked together, behind Mrs. Trent and Elizabeth. As they passed the steps leading down to the cellar on their way down the drive Elizabeth glanced involuntarily in their direction. wondering if Victor could hear them passng, and what he would be thinking. Mrs. Trent noticed how pale she looked this morning, and felt sad.

There was only just room for them all in the Priory pew. Elizabeth sat next to Julia and found it was a full time job keeping her place in the prayer book. She could read well, but not fast enough to cope with Cherubim and Seraphim and our forefather Abraham, sung very loudly and rapidly to the accompaniment of Miss Finch and the harmonium, yet she was greatly offended if an adult finger alighted on her book to point the place. Since she had been given her very own prayer book she would not accept even a temporary loan of anyone else's while her place was found, and Elizabeth's mind was kept from her troubles while she dealt with all these problems.

Brigadier Trent read the lessons. Julia felt proud as she watched the spare figure of her grandfather slowly mount the step up to the lectern. He stood, not unlike an eagle himself, above the brass bird on whose back rested the huge, ancient Bible, and slowly declaimed the prescribed words. Although he pretended it was only a tiresome duty, he really thoroughly enjoyed this weekly task. White bushy eyebrows waggling as he spoke, he read the story of Elijah being fed by the ravens, and his hearers listened in complete silence, even Julia sitting still to attend. When it came to the second lesson, what value he gave to the sounds he uttered. " ' Woe unto thee, Chorazin ! Woe unto thee, Bethsaida !' " he proclaimed, rolling the splendid syllables round his tongue. He looked what he was, a stern and upright man who could never tolerate or understand weakness in himself or in another.

Richard sat quietly listening while the Brigadier read. He had noticed Elizabeth's preoccupation with Julia and her prayer book; the church was not large, and the Trent's pew

was near the front, so he had also seen how white and strained
she looked. He felt more certain that she knew about Victor.

Church had a curious effect on Ivy. She was so cross with
Richard that she had intended not to come this morning, but
recently the choir had branched out into rather pretty cas-
socks and caps for the girls and she enjoyed wearing hers, so
in the end she relented. It was pleasant to stand, the cynosure,
she felt, of every eye, singing away, swathed in rich crimson
material. The whole thing was really rather nice, she thought,
like something in a film. All the people, tuneful or otherwise;
some of them drab and dowdy, but some ever so chic, like
young Mrs. Trent in her pink linen dress. How sad she looked,
a real Woman with a Past, she was. Then the little girl, quite
a cute little kid, really, peering over the top of the pew with
her big blue eyes. The Brigadier, too, what a character ! With
his white moustache and his fierce eyebrows he was like a
proper film lord. Mrs. Trent was a bit too pale and flustered
to stand up to comparisons with Hollywood, but it was true
she was a real nice lady, and always had a kind word if you
met her in the village. As for the vicar, though it would be
hard to forgive him for daring to criticise her, Ivy knew he'd
been put up to it by her Dad, and you couldn't deny but
that he was ever so romantic, with his limp and his smile, and
he always had such a nice clean freshly ironed surplice every
Sunday, not a thing like a crumpled handkerchief.

The hymns were nice : " Summer suns are glowing " was
cheerful and appropriate. Ivy sang with gusto, and wished
Alan was there to admire her. That was the worst of church,
you began to feel sentimental and imagine yourself floating
up the aisle all dressed in white satin, with orange blossom,
and bridesmaids in pink organdie, and Mr. Dell in his starched
surplice waiting to marry you at the other end, and everyone
turning round to say " Isn't she lovely," and " What a beautiful bride," as you passed. Even Alan might look quite nice in
his Air Force blue standing at the chancel steps.

But it was only a dream, of course." Reality was Harley
Darrell tomorrow, and the letter that had been secretly posted
to him last week.

Richard did not keep them long, and by ten to twelve everyone was filing slowly out into the sunshine. He took off his robes and went round to the porch to join in the leisurely chat as people greeted one another after the service. Talk was all of the lovely weather and whether it could possibly last. It was easy to say, " Here are the papers you asked for," and give Elizabeth the envelope, but there was no chance for further talk amongst so many people and it was with an anxious heart that Richard watched her walk away down the road, hand in hand with Julia.

IV

" Whatever did you have to go out for so suddenly, yesterday afternoon?" Mrs. Hopkins asked her policeman husband.

" That I cannot say, Daisy," he replied importantly.

" Someone run somebody over, I don't think," sniffed his wife, who was accustomed now to the trivial nature of Bramsbourne's crimes and had long given up hope of advancement for P.C. Hopkins. " I s'pose it was checking wireless licences again." She waited, hoping to lure some information out of the law's majesty, but in vain, and so perforce she returned to her household tasks.

Every Sunday morning in the summer P.C. Hopkins mowed his patch of lawn, and he was busy with this weekly labour when a large black car stopped outside his gate.

Sweating profusely, and out of breath, the stout constable welcomed any interruption. He mopped his streaming brow as he walked down the path.

" That's right, Hopkins, glad to see someone working," chuckled Inspector Howard, getting out of the car. " So you couldn't get on to anything in the village, eh?"

" No, sir," said Hopkins, standing to attention in his shirt sleeves. " Acting upon instructions received, sir, I proceeded at three-fifteen precisely into the village of Bramsbourne, where I made contact with—"

The inspector interrupted him. " You're not in court now, Hopkins, just tell me quickly who you saw."

The constable, hurt at having his eloquence cut short, listed the names of most of the villagers.

"I kept away from the Priory, as you said, sir," he continued, "but in the distance I saw the accused's—I mean young Mrs. Trent," he corrected himself, "proceeding in the general direction of the church, bearing a bunch of white daisies in 'er 'and. It's usual for the ladies of the village to take turns in harranging the flowers ready for the Sunday services," he kindly explained.

"I know, I know, get on," said the inspector impatiently.

"Some time later, I witnessed her return," the policeman resumed his tale, looking pained, "and later, I observed Brigadier Trent, and Mrs. Trent senior, and Miss Susan and 'er 'usband proceeding in Major Hugh Bellamy's green Jaguar motor car in the direction of the 'All, where last night 'is lordship held a cocktail party," he went on disapprovingly, as though he described a Borgia orgy. "I was later outside the 'ome of 'is lordship supervising the parking of the motor vehicles and ensuring that there was no obstruction to traffic wishing to pass along the road, and observed the party returning at eight o'clock."

"I see. And did you go to the Rose and Crown?" asked the inspector.

"Oh, no sir," exclaimed Hopkins in horror. "I never touch a drop, and it would have given rise to suspicion if I so much as put a foot inside such a place, unless to ascertain that no drinks were served after hours, which sort of behaviour Bert Higgs knows better than to attempt."

The inspector sighed. "And you didn't think of seeing they were keeping the rules last night? Never thought you'd hear a bit of talk if you went in on that excuse, eh?"

The constable dimly perceived that somehow he had disappointed his superior. "No, sir," he agreed in a puzzled voice.

"The saints preserve me from such numbskulls!" cried the inspector, raising his fists to heaven. "Well, there's nothing to be gained by standing here. We must go up to the Priory and make some enquiries."

"Oh, sir! Must I come?" asked Hopkins.

" Indeed you must come. Why not?" demanded Inspector Howard.

" Mrs. Trent's such a nice lady, and the Brigadier, I don't like to cause them trouble," explained the constable in bothered tones, with his face getting redder still in his distress.

" There's no time for sentiment in our job, as well you know, Hopkins," said the inspector brusquely. " Get yourself cleaned up and come along."

V

Nicholas, wearing only a diminutive pair of blue shorts, was running round and round in circles on the lawn in a mad fashion, pursuing some whim of his own, and watched in a resigned way by Rusty, who lay very still in the shade of a copper beech tree, with only his eyes moving as they ceaselessly followed the careering little figure. Susan was sitting in a deck-chair trying to read *The Sunday Times* and finding it difficult to control the large pages of the newspaper in her semi-prone position. Her peace was shattered by the sight of the police car driving up to the front door.

Guiltily she wondered if Rusty's licence had been remembered last January, forgetting that her home police would be more likely to enquire than P.C. Hopkins, whom she now recognised walking towards her, followed by two other men in uniform.

She laid her paper down on the grass and went to meet them, suddenly feeling afraid.

" Good morning," she greeted the constable, whom she had known since he arrived in Bramsbourne, a slim and ambitious young man, some fifteen years before.

" Good morning, Miss Susan, Mrs. Bellamy I mean," said Hopkins, looking extremely embarrassed. " This is Inspector Howard from Haverstoke, and Sergeant Wills," he announced gruffly, and stepped thankfully to the rear, handing the interview over to his superiors with relief.

" Good morning, Mrs. Bellamy," said the inspector, shaking hands.

"Good morning," said Susan enquiringly. Nicholas, fascinated by the spectacle of so many policemen, ran to her and stood on one leg, staring at them. Instinctively she reached for the comfort of his hot, sticky little hand.

"What a fine little chap. And what's your name?" asked the inspector, bending down. Nicholas went on staring in silence.

"Say 'Nicholas,'" Susan instructed automatically. I must keep calm, she was thinking, it's probably nothing.

"And how old are you?" the inspector bravely persisted.

"Eight," said Nicholas loudly.

Everyone laughed at such a gross mis-statement, and Susan began a long explanation about Julia being eight and Nicholas getting muddled. The inspector replied with a spirited account of his own child's failure to master the nine times table. Then an awkward, expectant hush fell.

Oh, do get on, get it over, Susan cried inwardly, let's know the worst.

"There are one or two things I want to ask you, madam, or your father if he's in," said the inspector at last, looking about him.

"Everyone else is at church," said Susan, and added, "Won't you come into the house?"

"Well, if we might, for five minutes," said the inspector.

A solemn procession filed towards the building.

In the drawing-room, everyone sat down, P.C. Hopkins lowering himself very gingerly on to a delicate carved chair that looked unequal to the load. Susan glanced at Nick.

"Run out and play, Nick, but keep near the house," she told him. "I'm nervous of the brook," she explained to the men.

"Hopkins will go with the young man," said Inspector Howard. "You like children, don't you, Hopkins?" he said brightly, and then to Nicholas, "You show all the flowers to the nice policeman." He grinned hugely as he watched his subordinate follow the tiny boy back out into the sunshine.

"Well, now, Inspector, what can I do for you?" asked Susan briskly.

"Mrs. Bellamy, I'm afraid I have a shock for you," said the inspector. "Your brother Victor Trent has escaped from Moorhurst Prison."

So it's true, thought Susan, her worst fears confirmed. The colour ebbed from her cheeks and she whispered, "Oh, no!"

"I don't want to distress you, Mrs. Bellamy. This must be painful for you," said the inspector, who in spite of his firm words to P.C. Hopkins had a sympathetic nature, which was one reason why he was a very successful policeman. "But naturally we must pick him up again as quickly as we can. He's been traced as far as Gloucester, since when we've lost track of him. It's possible he might be making in this direction, escaped convicts often visit their homes, either from sentiment or hoping to be hidden."

He looked shrewdly at the young woman. "Mrs. Bellamy, have you any reason to think your brother might be hiding in the vicinity?" he asked seriously.

Susan shook her head at once. Her blue eyes blazed indignantly as she said, "No, Inspector. And if he had turned up, I should have told you straight away. He's caused my family and his wife enough unhappiness without adding to it like this. Oh, why couldn't he have stayed quietly in prison?"

"He's been very foolish," agreed the inspector. Susan was either a consummate actress or genuinely appalled. He remembered the faint look of apprehension he had noticed when she greeted him, but that might be expected where there were in the past such unfortunate associations with the police.

"Please don't think I doubt your word, Mrs. Bellamy," he said gently. "I don't for a moment, but it's possible that he may be here unknown to yourself or your family. Would you have any objection if I take a look round? I haven't a warrant, so you're not obliged to agree, but if you refuse it will only mean that I shall return later with one, which will very likely add to your difficulties."

"Of course you can search," said Susan stoutly. "And if you find him you're welcome to him. Perhaps you think me very unfeeling and heartless, Inspector, but Victor has nearly killed my mother, shamed my father unbearably, and ruined the life of my sister-in-law. I was sorry for him, locked up in prison, but he deserved it, and if he can do this then I'm not any longer."

" I understand," said the inspector quietly. " We're bound to catch him in the end, for he can't lie up indefinitely; he'll need food and money and he'll give himself away eventually. Then he'll be worse off than he was before, for he'll lose his good conduct remission."

" Of course," said Susan thoughtfully. Food and money: Elizabeth had wanted money this morning. A dreadful suspicion began to form slowly in her mind. " I'll help you to look," she said.

It did not take long to search the house. They looked in every cupboard, under the beds, in the hall chest, and in the attic. Then they began on the garden; they examined the outhouses; they poked behind the oildrums and petrol cans in the garage; they combed the shrubbery, and they even looked between the rows of raspberries in the fruit cage.

The inspector scratched his head when all these places offered no clue, and smiled ruefully. " Well, it doesn't look as though he's got here yet," he said. " Oh, is there a cellar, Mrs. Bellamy? There's usually one in these old houses."

" Yes, there is," said Susan. " It's round here." She led the way past the rosebeds to the narrow paved path that led to where the cellar steps ran steeply down under the house. The inspector followed and clumpingly descended behind her.

The heavy oak door was stiff. " My parents don't use it in the summer, but the boiler for the central heating is in here," she explained, struggling to lift the latch.

" Here, let me," said the inspector. He gave the door a heave; it opened, and they went in.

Inspector Howard looked round. The only light came through the open door; there was nothing to be seen except the ghostly mounds of coke and the antiquated boiler, and on a ledge a pile of bulb bowls. A few loose pieces of coke were scattered about the floor.

" Smells, doesn't it?" commented the sergeant who had followed them.

" Hm, yes," said the inspector. He looked about him in a disappointed way. " There's no one here, though." He kicked the nearest pile of coke with his toe, and a shower of pieces cascaded down on to the flags; a film of dust hovered above them and slowly began to settle. The inspector turned, and stood aside for Susan to precede him up the stairs. At the door, he stopped and looked back again with a puzzled frown. There was something not quite right, but what was it? He shrugged; it must be just a fancy. Susan was waiting at the top of the stairs, and he slowly mounted to join her.

" Well, he isn't here," she said.

" No, and I hope he doesn't come, for your sake, Mrs. Bellamy," said the inspector.

" If I see him, you shall know at once," she promised.

" Good." Inspector Howard smiled. " We shall have to keep a watch on all roads, of course, so he's not likely to get through."

" Must my mother and father know about this?" asked Susan. " I suppose they'll have to later, but they've been looking forward so much to this weekend, and having us all to stay; need they be told yet?"

" Well, it will be in all the papers," the inspector pointed out. " They're sure to give his name and description. But perhaps there's a chance your parents won't notice it, and I see no reason why you should tell them we've been this morning, if you prefer not to."

" Oh, thank you, Inspector," said Susan gratefully. " What about the other man? Is he still free?"

" No, they picked him up early today outside London," said Inspector Howard.

Susan glanced at her watch. " Would you mind hurrying if you really are ready to leave," she begged. " The others will be back from church in a few minutes and if they see you I shall have to explain."

" No, we'll get along now," he said. " Come along, Sergeant." Inwardly his well-trained mind registered the fact that Susan had known there was a second man with her brother, which was a piece of information he had not given her.

"Don't worry too much, Mrs. Bellamy," he said aloud, "Will try to keep it as quiet as we can for the moment. We don't want a lot of commotion."

"I'm so grateful; thank you," said Susan. "Goodbye."

Inspector Howard returned to his car, and with his sergeant at the wheel was borne away. When they were half-way back to Haverstoke they remembered that they had abandoned P.C. Hopkins at the Priory, heatedly pushing Nick on the swing, with no transport home except his legs. The inspector laughed heartily at this for the rest of the journey to the police station. P.C. Hopkins did not think it so amusing as he trudged back for one mile in the hot midday sun.

Susan had plenty to think about as she returned to her deck chair. Elizabeth's request for money had certainly been very strange, yet there was no sign here of Victor, so how could she have wanted it for him? Anyway if he did turn up, she would give herself the satisfaction of telling him just what she thought of him before she gave him up. However, it was to be hoped he would be recaptured quickly, before the news of his escape spread any further.

Down in the cellar, Victor heard the police car start up and drive away, as earlier he had heard it arrive. Almost suffocated, he burrowed out from under the mound of coke with which he had frantically buried himself when he had heard P.C. Hopkins' booming, unmistakable voice in the garden. He dragged out with him the now filthy rug, and the thermos flask. His heart pounded with fright. He had felt like a snared animal when Inspector Howard's foot had kicked against his covering.

Victor took the heavy key from his pocket and locked himself in again; he looked as black and dirty as a chimney sweep.

The dark atmosphere of the cellar was heavy with dust from the disturbed coke.

VI

Alan Blake sat brooding in the living-room of his friend Jeff Parke's married quarters, where he spent much of his free time. How pleasant it would be if he could live in such a charming home, with Ivy to share it, he thought wistfully. Jeff's wife, Mabel, heavily pregnant, sang cheerfully as she carried in the Sunday dinner. Just so would Ivy sing and be gay in similar circumstances, he dreamed, forgetting that she might be far more likely to grumble and complain unceasingly.

"What's on your mind, lad?" asked Jeff kindly, exchanging a meaning look with his wife. "Still worrying about the girl friend?"

Alan nodded unhappily.

"The course of true love never runs smooth," pronounced Mabel. "Cheer up, Alan; Rome wasn't built in a day, you know."

She went into the tiny kitchen to fetch the gravy, and in spite of his depression Alan smiled; Mabel Parke was famous for her habit of quoting proverbs, and she thrived on the teasing this provoked.

"Wondering when to pop the question, eh?" asked Jeff, noisily sharpening the carving knife.

Alan said dejectedly, "I've popped it, Jeff, and she didn't half turn me down flat."

"Well, you are a one," said Jeff unsympathetically. "Always rushing your fences, you are."

"Poor Alan," said Mabel, with more compassion than her husband. She lowered herself into a chair, and sighed with relief for her legs were aching. "Never mind," she went on cheerfully, "'If at first you don't succeed, try, try, try again.' She's likely only teasing you. Why don't you bring her over here for tea one day? When she sees how nice we live, and meets a few of your friends, she'll surely think again."

"Thanks, Mabel, you're a sport," said Alan gratefully. "Maybe I will at that." He started wondering what Ivy would think about Mabel, and unwillingly began to see her in a different light. With her round, unpowdered face, her homely pinafore, and her always plump, now overburdened body, she was in sharp contrast to the slim sophistication of Ivy. He thought of her harsh words on the river about having babies and getting ugly; somehow he felt the meeting would not help his cause, yet Mabel and Jeff were two of the best people he knew. It was a hopeless situation; like Mark Antony he longed to be free from the fetters of love, yet lacked the power to cast them off. He sighed heavily.

"Come on, Alan, your dinner will be cold," said Mabel briskly. "It can't be as bad as all that. All girls want to get married some day, you know, and who could she find that's nicer than you, I'd like to know? She's very young, isn't she, nineteen did you say? P'raps she's not ready for a lot of responsibility yet." She looked complacently down at her own portentous form. "Another year or so, and likely she'll feel different."

"Maybe," said Alan without much hope. "But I may have been moved by then." He began to attack his roast beef without enthusiasm. "She thinks I'm too dull," he told them.

"Dull, indeed," said Jeff with a laugh. "She should see you in the mess when you get going. Dull, did she say? Well, I never!" He spanked his thigh, chuckling to himself. Alan was famous in the sergeants' mess for his life-like impersonations of some of the officers, but he needed a lot of persuading to give them. "And aren't you one of the best pilots in the group? Better tell her so." He stuffed his mouth full of crisp roast potato and Yorkshire pudding.

Alan chewed slowly. It was true, but if he told her, Ivy would never believe it; she would only jeer as she had on Saturday. He would have to convince her of his abilities in some other way.

"Anyway, whoever you marry, you'll never find a cook to touch Mabel," Jeff declared with pride.

Mabel blushed with pleasure and hit her husband fondly on the back. "Get along with you, Jeff," she said happily. "Now, then, Alan, have some more Yorkshire pudding. You must keep your pecker up, you know."

VII

Miss Finch, who on Sundays played the harmonium in church and on weekdays ran Bramsbourne's post office, was sitting in her back garden reading *Her Dream Fulfilled* with eager eyes. Though well past forty, she still hoped a Prince Charming would one day come and whisk her away from her wooden counter and her stamps to a red brick bungalow, which was her up-to-date ideal of a castle; and while she waited for him to appear, she fed herself vicarious romance through the medium of lurid tales of love and passion.

She started when Elizabeth came round the side of her cottage, and her spectacles slipped off her nose.

" Oh, Miss Finch, did I give you a fright?" Elizabeth asked. " I'm so sorry, I did knock but perhaps you didn't hear."

" That's quite all right, Mrs. Trent," said Miss Finch, hastily hiding her book behind her back as she stood up, for its wrapper displayed a sultry blonde in a rather abandoned attitude.

" I'm sorry to disturb you, and on a Sunday too," Elizabeth went on. " But I wondered if you would be kind enough to cash a cheque for me."

" Well," said Miss Finch hesitantly, while she thought. Such things were against her rules, but young Mrs. Trent was ever such a nice lady, held in high regard by all the village, and surely it was only right to help her if she could. " I'd be pleased to," she decided, " but I haven't got a lot of money here. It's the weekend you see, and by the time I've paid the allowances on Friday I get short." She stood aside for Elizabeth to enter the white-painted cottage. " Come along in, if you will, Mrs. Trent, and I'll see what I can do."

Elizabeth ducked her head to go through the low doorway. Inside it was dark after the bright sunlight, and she screwed up her eyes. Miss Finch showed her into the post office room which was at the front and unlocked her money drawer.

" I was so stupid and forgot to bring any money away with me," said Elizabeth, feeling that some explanation was due.

" Of course, we all forget things sometimes," said Miss Finch tolerantly. Elizabeth's tragic past lent her glamour, and people with unmentionable secrets must be allowed a little absent-mindedness. On the whole Miss Finch decided that her own virgin life was preferable to Elizabeth's chequered wedlock. Scuffling in her drawer of papers, the postmistress hid her gaudy novel under a pile of forms and began to count the money.

"Three pounds, four shillings and fivepence halfpenny," she announced. "You could have two pounds ten, Mrs. Trent. I must keep some for when we reopen after the holiday."

"Thank you, that will do beautifully, Miss Finch," said Elizabeth, hiding her dismay at such a small amount. "I'm only so sorry to bother you." She opened her bag and quickly wrote out the cheque.

"Don't mention it, I'm sure, Mrs. Trent," said Miss Finch. Poor young lady, she thought, how white and tired she looks. It must be dreadful to know that *he* is inside. The little spinster shuddered inwardly. Still, with a good woman beside him, young Victor would surely go straight when at last the price was paid. She sighed emotionally as she relocked the drawer.

"What a nice service it was this morning," she said conversationally, leading Elizabeth back out into the garden. "Do excuse me taking you round the back way, but the front door is all bolted up till after the holiday."

"Of course. Yes, it was lovely," Elizabeth agreed. "How pretty your garden looks, Miss Finch. You'll be winning all the prizes tomorrow."

Miss Finch beamed with pleasure. "That's what the vicar says," she said. "What a fine man he is, we are lucky to have him. He makes the services go with such a swing, if you know what I mean."

"Yes, indeed," said Elizabeth. She smiled, thinking that Richard would be amused to hear this description.

"And you play so beautifully, too," she added tactfully.

Miss Finch glowed. "That's very kind, I'm sure," she said modestly. "It's a pleasure, really, when the vicar is so helpful." Unspoken and adverse criticism of the departed Reverend Clark, now sweltering in Darkest Africa, hovered between the two ladies. "And the choir is so keen too, all the boys and girls are ever so conscientious," continued Miss Finch enthusiastically. "Only I do wish Mr. Dell would speak to Ivy

Higgs, such a guy she looks, with all that powder, and she Uses Scent." This could only mean one thing to Miss Finch. The faint fragrance of Elizabeth was in quite another category. "But he's too patient," she went on in a fond voice.

"It does seem a pity she should spoil her looks," agreed Elizabeth. "But so many girls overdo it when they first grow up. She'll give it up when she marries and settles down. She's got a young man, hasn't she?"

"Oh, yes, and he's ever so nice," said Miss Finch, for was not Alan a cavalier of the skies? "Well, perhaps we shall have wedding bells ringing out any day. That would be nice. We haven't had a wedding for three months."

"It must be lovely to play the organ for weddings," said Elizabeth. "You must enjoy helping to make the day happy for everyone." She smiled at the little woman.

"Oh, I do, and it's so romantic," said Miss Finch earnestly.

"We had no music when I was married," said Elizabeth. Her thoughts flew back to the cold, almost empty church, where she and Victor had been bound irrevocably together by a clergyman who knew neither of them, hundreds of miles away from his family and with her own parents dead. "That was in the war, of course," she added. "Well, I mustn't keep you any longer, Miss Finch. Thank you so much again. Goodbye." So saying, she went away down the path, and Miss Finch looked after her admiringly. Well, fancy her coming out with it straight like that, about her own wedding, she thought, dumbfounded. You had to admit it took nerve to do that, when most people would never want to speak about such an unlucky day. Miss Finch sighed again, and went into her cottage once more to fetch *Her Dream Fulfilled*.

Outside in the road Elizabeth's cheerful smile disappeared. Two pounds ten shillings was not going to take Victor very far. She had only managed to collect twenty-one pounds, ten shillings. Certainly Brigadier and Mrs. Trent would have some money between them, but if she asked for it they would be sure to think it as odd as Susan had done. There was still the village shop, Brown's Emporium, as it was grandly called, where she might be able to cash another cheque.

Mr. Brown conducted his business in a gaunt grey cement building, with a corrugated iron extension at one side for the new lines he stocked. As it was Sunday the blinds were drawn in the windows, and Elizabeth was spared the tantalising display of patent medicines, under wear and groceries which were normally to be seen herded unsuitably together to lure the unwary window-shopper.

Mr. Brown came to the door after her third knock, by which time she was wishing she had never thought of trying him. He made a great clatter unbolting the door from within, and somewhat sulkily agreed to supply ten pounds.

Elizabeth loathed herself and Victor too as she thankfully took the money and went away. Miss Finch had been so pleasant, but Mr. Brown's begrudging manner filled her with distaste for her task.

Thirty-one pounds was a lot of money, but if it came to heavy bribes it would not last long. Thank goodness she had got plenty in the bank, her precious savings, to meet this sudden demand. It was nearly four o'clock; there was just time before tea to go to the Rose and Crown. Mr. Higgs would be sure to have money in hand after Saturday night; that, she understood, was the big night of the week for publicans.

The inn was closed, but Bert Higgs was polishing his bar counter and through the window he saw Elizabeth coming. He let her in by the side door and led her to his own sitting-room, where Ivy reclined on a settee, embedded in *Scandals of the Screen*. Elizabeth could not help smiling; Miss Finch's choice of literature had not escaped her notice; despite the postmistress's disapproval of Ivy their taste was not so very different.

The young girl jumped up when she saw who the visitor was, shaking her heavy hair back from her face. She pulled a chair forward, for she approved of Elizabeth and so honoured her with her best manners.

"Do sit down, Mrs. Trent," said Ivy politely.

"You'll have a cup of tea, madam, of course," said Bert, with a meaning look at his daughter, before Elizabeth could explain her errand.

" I'd love one, if you're making it," said Elizabeth, touched by how obviously pleased they were to see her, unlike Mr. Brown. She wondered if it was merely because they pitied her, and hoped that it was not. While Ivy went uncomplainingly away to brew the tea, she embarked on a long conversation with Bert Higgs about tomorrow's excitements, and found it difficult to get round to the object of her visit.

" Why, certainly, madam, I'll gladly cash a cheque," agreed Bert at once. " Funny you should ask, vicar was here this morning for the very same thing. But I've plenty left, I always believe in having money in the house. You never know when you'll need it suddenly." He went off to fetch his tin box, and Elizabeth was left alone. Richard must have taken the trouble to come all the way down here this morning to get that money for her, she realised.

The big leather chair was comfortable and she was very tired; it was a relief to relax. She began to feel drowsy and closed her eyes, pretending for a foolish moment that she was married to Richard and out visiting as a vicar's wife should. The return of Ivy, bearing the tea, brought her back to the very different truth, and she sat up with a start.

" Here you are, Mrs. Trent; sugar?" asked Ivy, smiling pleasantly. She had brought a small tray, laid with a spotless cloth and the best china. Two wafer-thin slices of bread and butter reposed triangular-wise on a plate.

" Oh, Ivy, how sweet of you to take so much trouble," exclaimed Elizabeth in warm appreciation, forbearing to remark that a vast tea awaited her at the Priory.

Ivy beamed; she had not touched her face since before church that morning, and much of her armour of paint had worn off; consequently she looked her best.

" It's a pleasure," said she, and meant it.

Elizabeth sipped the strong tea, and sought about in her mind for something to say.

" When are you getting married, Ivy?" she asked.

Ivy pouted. " I'm not getting married," she said.

" Oh, I'm sorry; I had an idea you were," said Elizabeth. The longing to unburden herself to somebody suddenly became too much for Ivy, and she said in a burst of confidence, "Well, he has asked me, but I said no."

"Did you?" Elizabeth was good with people, and she was not so engrossed with her own misfortune that she failed to recognise Ivy's pent-up state. She waited expectantly, wearing an encouraging expression.

"I don't want to be married yet, I want some fun," the girl burst out. "I'm young, why shouldn't I go to Hollywood and be a film star? I'm just as pretty as Delia Dymple."

Elizabeth struggled between dismay and amusement.

"You are indeed," she agreed. "Prettier, in fact. And you could have a lot of fun without going to Hollywood. You'd be silly to get married if you aren't in love with your young man, but I thought he looked so nice." She stopped, wondering if she would be told any more.

"Well, yes, he is nice, I suppose," Ivy admitted reluctantly. "But he's not very exciting, not a bit like Harley Darrell on the films."

Elizabeth smiled. "I don't suppose he is," she agreed, "and Harley Darrell isn't nearly so exciting off the screen, though he's very nice too."

"Do you *know* him, Mrs. Trent?" gasped Ivy, round-eyed with amazement. Elizabeth nodded, and thought ruefully that she had said the wrong thing. Ivy's next words confirmed that suspicion.

"Oh, Mrs. Trent, will you introduce me to him tomorrow? Oh, say you will, please say you will," she begged, hands clasped in entreaty.

Elizabeth looked at her consideringly. "Yes, Ivy, I will, if you really want me to," she said slowly, "but don't think he'll whisk you back to Hollywood with him. He's always meeting girls who want him to do just that." This was pure surmise on Elizabeth's part, but it was near enough to the truth for her purpose, which was to discourage Ivy.

"Oh, but he might, Mrs. Trent, and anyway I would have done my best to make him," Ivy declared.

Elizabeth knew very well that although it was unlikely in the extreme for Hollywood to choose Ivy when they must have thousands of pretty girls applying to them daily, it was still possible for them to groom her for stardom and change her personality into any shape or form, if the fancy took them.

She said, " I don't think you'd find being on the films much fun, you know. It's very hard work; up at five very often, and home late."

" But look at how rich they are, and famous," said Ivy. " People always saying how wonderful they are !" Her eyes opened wide at the thought of such success.

" Isn't it enough if one nice, honest young man thinks you're wonderful?" asked Elizabeth gently. Her own life was in such a muddle that at the risk of being interfering she could not refrain from trying to help the girl sort out her confusion.

Ivy's lip drooped. " But he's dull," she repeated, though more doubtfully.

Outside the door, Bert Higgs heard their conversation and decided that Elizabeth was more than earning her cup of tea. He tiptoed away; it would be a mistake to interrupt them; Mrs. Trent could have the money when she had finished her chat with Ivy.

" But Ivy, real life isn't at all like the films," Elizabeth was saying. She thought of Victor lurking in the cellar, the mobilised policemen searching for him, and her own dramatic position, and almost laughed, for here were the ingredients for a stirring few reels. Aloud she continued, " I don't think we would be very happy if we lived the sort of life they show in most films, with quarrels all the time, or fights and gangsters, and people running away with other people's wives and husbands. Real life offers us more than that, if we're lucky, and if we get our opportunity at the right moment." She thought with longing of Richard and the full life she could have shared with him. Her unhappiness spurred her on to try and make Ivy understand. She continued gently, " Nature meant us to marry and have babies." Suddenly, for the first time, she realised that if Victor's escape succeeded she would be reprieved. She paused for a moment, and then brought her mind back to what she had been saying. " Perhaps you don't care enough for your airman to marry him, but one day you will meet someone whom you will be able to love. Don't miss your chance when it comes, Ivy."

The girl looked at her uncertainly. Surely someone who was as much at home in the sophistication of Mayfair as in the rusticity of Bramsbourne should know what she was talking about, thought Ivy confusedly.

"Did you quarrel, after you'd turned your young man down?" asked Elizabeth.

"Mm, yes, in a sort of way," admitted Ivy. "I was awful," she confessed, "I didn't ought to have been so cruel." Now, just as they had last night, tears sprang unfamiliarly into her large brown eyes.

"Well, you'll be seeing him again soon, won't you? You must say you're sorry," said Elizabeth gently. "Or write to him. If he's fond of you, he'll forgive you."

"P'raps I will," said Ivy.

"I should," Elizabeth said. "You think about it."

Ivy nodded unhappily. She glanced at Elizabeth, whose clear, pale skin bore only the lightest dusting of powder, and whose lips were delicately touched with red. There was no similarity between her skilful aids to nature and Ivy's heavy-handed disguise. A whole hosts of hitherto unthought-of ideas began to form in her obtuse mind.

"It's been ever so good of you, Mrs. Trent," she said awkwardly, and dashed the back of her hand against her still brimming eyes.

"That's all right, Ivy. It often helps to talk things over with somebody." Elizabeth felt some compunction as she saw the unhappiness in the girl's expression, but perhaps this was the first step towards a more sensible frame of mind, and she hoped her advice had been right. She was relieved when Mr. Higgs came into the room with a bundle of banknotes in his hand.

"Ivy and I have had such a nice talk," she said, feeling some remark was expected.

"That's very kind of you, Mrs. Trent," said Bert. He glanced curiously at his daughter, whose face was turned away. "Ivy's a good girl, but she's got her head full of a lot of nonsense," he said, and earned himself an unfilial glare. "Here's the money you were wanting, fifteen pounds," he said, and began to count it slowly out.

"It is kind of you, Mr. Higgs; I'm very grateful," said Elizabeth. She put the money in her bag and got up. "Thank you very much for the tea, Ivy," she said.

When she had gone, Ivy asked her father in roundeyed wonder, "Surely Mrs. Trent won't spend all that money tomorrow at the Flower Show, will she?"

"That's got nothing to do with you, my girl," said Bert. "Mrs. Trent's affairs are her own business entirely, and no concern of anyone else." Upon which stern pronouncement he stalked from the room to complete his polishing of the bar.

VIII

Though the police had apparently been satisfied that he had not reached the Priory, Victor in his cellar was a very frightened man. They would be watching for him on all the roads in the district; by now they might have contacted the fair people who had given him a lift and who would be sure to report what they had done. Yesterday it had been exciting, rather like a game of dares, skulking about in the bushes and getting home without being seen, a challenge to his nerve, just as falsifying accounts had been a challenge to his skill. The young man and the girl in the meadow might have spotted him, but luckily they had been too much occupied with each other to gaze at the view.

He had spent some hours hiding in the leafy bushes of the churchyard, and had been astonished to see Elizabeth. He had no idea that she was on such friendly terms with the parson, but there was no mistaking the look on both their faces when they supposed themselves alone. It was the typical criminal's conceit and urge for power that had caused Victor to quit the comparative safety of the cellar and confront Richard this morning, just to see what effect his appearance would have. The money would be useful too, if Richard decided to bring it. Victor was not so foolish that he did not recognise an upright man when he saw one, and he knew that Richard would attach no importance to his blackmailing threats, except in so far as they would affect Elizabeth; and this concern for her would also, Victor was certain, prevent him telling the police. But now he had let himself in for another dangerous journey back to the church, perhaps to be caught. He began to fear that his adventure was not going to succeed, and he quailed at the grim thought of returning to prison. No conquering hero would he be then, but simply another mug who'd got nabbed.

He wondered how late it was; he was hungry and uncomfortable, and he longed for Elizabeth to appear with a report of the situation above ground and some food. She was just as lovely as ever, and he was genuinely distressed at the grief he had brought her. Forgetting the church's view on divorce, he supposed she would marry that parson fellow in the end. Well, he looked a decent chap, he would be a respectable sort of husband and make her happy, which goodness knew she deserved. He just mustn't get caught again, for that would put the lid on her getting a divorce. What a pity she hadn't done it when he was first locked up, but she was so idealistic, wanting to have another try at keeping him straight. Victor laughed at himself. He hadn't stolen only because he was short of money; there had been excitement in deceiving his victims for so long, just as now there was a certain thrill in knowing that hundreds of policemen were busy on his account.

His body pricked with the dust that had worked its way down inside his clothes. Somehow he would have to get cleaned up before he attempted to travel any further. It was very uncomfortable sitting on the coke, in spite of his rug, and the air was dank and oppressive. Though he was warm enough, Victor shivered.

IX

Richard still could not decide what to do. Clearly the proper course was to inform the police of his meeting with Victor so that they could surround the churchyard and surprise him

when he came to collect the money. But it was an incontro-
vertible fact that if he was captured further away from Bramsbourne the Trents would escape with less publicity and distress
than if he was found almost on their doorstep.

Then, too, if as he feared Elizabeth did indeed know of
Victor's presence in the neighbourhood and had not reported
it, might she not find herself in trouble with the police?
Richard was uncertain of the law, but it could scarcely condone
the concealment of a criminal. However, it was possible that
Elizabeth's pallor was only due to hearing of the escape
through the paper, or perhaps the police had already questioned her. Whichever way you looked at it, it was still curious
that she had wanted so much money.

Richard wondered where Victor had gone after he left the
church this morning; no doubt it was better not to know his
hiding place. Whatever happened, he was unlikely to get far
away from Bramsbourne for all roads were sure to be watched.
Even if they were unaware of it, the Trents were in great
trouble, and Richard at last made up his mind to go to the
Priory and see if all was well.

He walked quickly through the village which seemed almost
deserted in the heat. A few children played hop-scotch in the
road and a cat slumbered peacefully under the shade of a
thick hedge, otherwise all was still. Brigadier Trent was sitting
on an upturned box, weeding. He was pleased to see Richard,
whom he found a refreshing change from the departed Reverend Clark, and buttonholed him in conversation. They discussed the sports arrangements for the Flower Show, for the
Brigadier was the official starter for these important events.
Certainly he seemed his usual self, thought Richard in some
relief, glad that he was obviously unaware of what had happened.

Mrs. Trent heard voices and came round the side of the
house. "Hullo, Richard," she said, "come and see my
gladioli. I want your opinion on whether they're better than
the Favershams'." He followed her across the lawn to where
they grew in a wide bed in a profusion of colour. They were
certainly splendid.

"Yours should win easily," he said at once. "They're superb."

Mrs. Trent smiled. "They're the best we've had for some years," she said. "I was afraid they wouldn't be out in time, but this sun has brought them on perfectly. I shall cut them tonight."

She too appeared quite calm. They walked along, admiring the roses which in the heat were turning from tight buds into full blown cabbages in a single day.

"I don't know where Elizabeth is," said Mrs. Trent. "She disappeared some time ago. Perhaps she's gone for a walk. I don't think she looks very well, do you, Richard?"

"She looked pale in church, I thought," he agreed. "Perhaps she finds the hot weather trying?" he suggested. He could not enlighten Mrs. Trent as to what he thought must be the real reason when she herself seemed quite undisturbed.

"I think she enjoys the warm weather as a rule," said Mrs. Trent. "I expect she's been working too hard." She broke a dead head from a marigold. "I love these," she went on, "if you keep cutting off the withered ones they last all the summer and autumn, and they're so cheerful, like Susan. She should have been called Marigold."

Richard laughed. "I expect she thinks Susan is a prettier name," he said.

"Stay to tea, Richard," suggested Mrs. Trent. "Elizabeth will be back then, and she will be so sorry to miss you."

"Thank you," said Richard, and as he knew her invitation was sincere he did not embark on a host of polite protestations.

"Where's Aunt Beth?" asked Julia, running up to them, with Rusty skipping round her in excited circles, full of energy in spite of the heat. "She said she'd play hide-and-seek this afternoon."

"I'll play instead, if you like," offered Richard.

"Oh will you, goody!" cried the little girl, and added confidentially, "I didn't think parsons could run."

Richard laughed. "Well, perhaps not as fast as you," he said, "but nearly as fast as Daddy."

Julia asked, " Even with your wooden leg?"

" Julia!" cried Mrs. Trent in shocked reproof.

" Even with my wooden leg," said Richard solemnly. " As a matter of fact, it isn't wood, it's tin. You can see it if you like. It's very clever, it wears a shoe and sock just like my proper one." Obligingly he hitched up the end of his trouser-leg to display the limb to her interested gaze.

" Hm," Julia was not impressed. " It would be much more fun if you had a stick one, like Long John Silver," she said disparagingly, " with a little bit of rubber on the end like the man who begs outside the post office at home."

" I'm sorry you don't like Timothy," said Richard in a disappointed voice. " He's very useful to me, much more useful than a peg-leg would be."

" Timothy! Is that what you call it?" asked the little girl with more interest. " Why does it have a name?"

" It's very human, like one of your dolls, so it must have a name," Richard told her. " It comes off at night, you know, and sleeps on its own special shelf. Then it has to be dressed every day to match the other leg."

" However do you do it? Do you hop about zipping it on?" asked Julia.

" Well, usually I sit," said Richard solemnly. " You see it hasn't got a zip, only buckles."

" Fancy!" Julia looked at him with respect. " Well, let's start the game. You hide first and I'll be ' he.' Come on Nick, go and hide with Mr. Dell."

Richard removed his jacket and hung it on a tree. Then he took the little boy's hand and they went away to hide behind the greenhouse. Soon shrieks of delight rang out as they dodged round it with Julia in pursuit and Rusty barking encouragement.

Richard was rather warm when at last the summons to tea reprieved him. " Poor Richard, you must be exhausted," said Mrs. Trent. " You've certainly earned your tea."

" I enjoyed it," said Richard, rumpling Nick's untidy hair. " We made Julia run, didn't we, Nick?"

Nick, whose method of hiding was to conceal his head

only, in the fond belief that because he could not see, his own
stout person must also be invisible, nodded emphatically.
"Me can run so fast," he declared proudly.

Tea was laid in the dining-room. Hugh arrived blinking,
having spent a blissful afternoon at the furthest end of the
garden from his noisy offspring, sound asleep in a deckchair,
and Susan came in talking very fast.

"Mummy, you haven't got a hat that's fit to be seen, what
are you going to wear tomorrow? Hullo, Richard, I didn't see
you. Come along, Nick and Julia, sit down quietly. Well,
Hugh, had a good afternoon?" she said, breathlessly.

Mrs. Trent replied calmly to the first part of her remarks.

"I have my best navy straw, and it's perfectly fit to be
seen, and may I ask what you've been doing with my hats
anyway?"

"What, that old thing? You can't wear that again,"
declared Susan with scorn. "You've worn it every single year
for the Flower Show since you bought it for our wedding."

"Well, as you've pointed out, I've nothing else suitable,
so it must do," said her mother equably. "It was most expensive and it will still look good."

"Mummy, you're hopeless. You really might get a new hat
once in a few years," said Susan. "Perhaps Elizabeth could
modernise it for you, she's good at that sort of thing." She
looked round in surprise, suddenly aware that her sister-in-law
was missing. "Wherever is she?" she asked.

"I'm here," said Elizabeth, appearing in the doorway. "I'm
so sorry to be late, I didn't notice the time."

"You haven't said why you were interfering with Granny's
hats, Mummy," said Julia, enchanted with an opportunity of
seeing her parent discomfited.

"I was seeing if you had any decent flowers I could borrow
for mine," said Susan, without shame.

Everyone laughed, and Elizabeth said, "Well, I wasn't
going to wear a hat. Must one?"

"Your hair's so nice, you don't need one," said Susan, "but
when you're fat and middle-aged like me you look undressed
without," she added.

"Well, if you're middle-aged, I must be ready for a bath-chair," said Mrs. Trent.

"Middle-aged, indeed," grunted Hugh, helping himself to chocolate cake, "what rubbish you talk Sue."

"I'm thirty-four; that's what they call in books a woman who has passed her youth," insisted Susan.

Elizabeth laughed. "Well, if you're middle-aged, then I must be too," she said, "so we'd better all wear hats."

"We'll have a hat parade after tea," said Susan. "We must make Mummy presentable tomorrow, Elizabeth. Lady Faversham is sure to be a knock-out in Dior's latest, so you must keep your own end up, Mummy."

Elizabeth glanced quickly at Susan across the table. Though she was renowned as the wag of the family there was something false about her efforts to amuse now, a sort of near-hysterical undercurrent to her excited voice. Their eyes met, and Susan at once looked away. On the occasions in her life when she had needed courage, Susan had always found plenty, but this time it was lacking. As far as she knew, of all the people gathered so lightheartedly round the table, she alone was aware of Victor's escape, and she could not bear the burden of her secret. As soon as there was a chance to speak privately to Hugh, she must tell him; she would let him know also about Elizabeth asking for money, and he would decide whether it was possible for Victor to have communicated with her, and if so, what to do about it.

Richard glanced at Elizabeth. If she really had seen Victor or heard from him, she was putting up a marvellous show, he thought, hearing her embarking now on a discussion of fashion with every appearance of absorption. He did not know. Susan well enough to detect the nervousness behind her chatter, but presently he saw Elizabeth, who was normally so neat and precise in everything she did, knock some of her tea into her saucer with a small flurried movement. Sensing that he watched her, she gave him a faint smile; it was comforting to be near him, even though she could not tell him of her anxiety, for he would in duty be obliged to report Victor.

Richard had to hurry back to the Vicarage in time for his

evening service with no chance of seeing her alone and with his worry unabated.

After tea, Susan still insisted on the hat inspection, so Mrs. Trent and Elizabeth trooped upstairs with her, followed by Julia and Nick. Susan scornfully spread out her mother's modest array of millinery upon the bed. One particularly sombre model in black felt she put upon her own head at an angle very different from that intended by the designer twenty years before, and went into peals of laughter at her appearance.

"Why do you keep them for so long, Mummy?" she asked. "Don't you ever give them to the jumble sales?"

"It isn't meant to be worn like that, Susan," said Mrs. Trent mildly. She removed it from her daughter's head. "This is how it should be put on," she announced, pulling it well forward over her nose. "You'll learn one day that everything comes back into fashion if you keep it long enough."

"Well, it looks funnier still like that," said Susan, unabashed.

Meanwhile Nicholas had found Mrs. Trent's elderly fox fur in the cupboard, and now he strutted round the room singing loudly, wearing it draped like a priest's stole, trailing over his shoulders to the floor, and with his grandmother's despised best navy straw hat, complete with veiling, on his head at a jaunty angle.

Elizabeth quickly rescued the hat and exchanged it for the black felt they had just been discussing, which she agreed with Susan could well be spared from Mrs. Trent's wardrobe. She snipped the veiling neatly off before there was time to protest and put the straw upon her mother-in-law's silver hair.

"We'll put the ribbon from this other hat on it, like this," she said, deftly twining it round the crown. "Now it just needs a stitch to hold it firm and it looks quite different. Everyone will think you've spent fifteen guineas in Bond Street," she declared.

Mrs. Trent did not mind what anyone thought, but as the swiftest way of gaining peace was to suffer uncomplainingly her family's ministrations until they were satisfied, she acquiesced, and thanked Elizabeth for her efforts.

Julia, who had been quietly enjoying herself trying on one hat after the other, first the right way round and then back to front, now asked, " Mummy, *can* I have my hair cut, please?"

" We'll see, Julia, I've told you I'll think about it," answered Susan impatiently, deciding, sadly that Elizabeth's smart hat which she so much admired only emphasised the roundness of her own plump face.

" 'We'll see,' that's all you ever say," mimicked Julia rudely. " Come on Nick," she shouted, and rushed from the room, deaf to the scolding voice that called her back. Sensing trouble, Nick followed her at speed, still wearing his grandmother's hat.

" Leave her, Sue, she's over-excited," pleaded Mrs. Trent, as Susan set off in pursuit. " In any case, why don't you let her have it off? It would be far less trouble."

Susan came slowly back into the room. " I expect I will," she said, " but she mustn't speak like that just because she can't have her own way immediately."

They began to put the hats away, and outside in the garden Julia, with her rage forgotten, persuaded her father and grandfather to resume the game of hide-and-seek begun with Richard earlier.

" Mind, no peeping, Daddy," she warned sternly, leaving the reluctant Hugh counting to a hundred while they hid. She looked about for a good place; Grandfather, to save himself trouble, had nipped behind the holly hedge.

" I know, let's hide in the cellar," she said eagerly, and seized Nick's hand. " Come on."

They crept down the steep steps in their rubber-soled sandals, Nick clutching hard at the banister rail, game enough for any adventure. Julia stood on her tiptoes to reach the doorlatch. She struggled with it but it would not move.

" It's awfully stiff," she said. " Oh, well, never mind. It's rather horrid and spooky in there anyway. We'll try somewhere else."

Victor heard the children's voices growing fainter as they

went away, and relaxed again. It was clammy and airless in the cellar; he felt as though the ceiling was pressing on his head. Soon, however risky it would be, he must open the door for some air.

X

It was later in the evening : upstairs Susan and Elizabeth were putting the children to bed; downstairs Brigadier Trent was reading the paper; outside the garage Hugh was tinkering with the carburettors of his car, one of his favourite pastimes. Carrying her secateurs and gardening-basket, Mrs. Trent went into the garden to gather her flowers ready for the Flower Show tomorrow.

The delphiniums were nearly over, but by careful selection she could find enough tall spikes to give height to a bowl of mixed flowers. She moved slowly round the garden, methodically choosing what she wanted, and carrying her choice to a bucket of water that she had already put in the shade of the porch. Here they would spend the night, and in the morning she would arrange them in the marquee. There were plenty of sweet peas, growing like soldiers on parade in straight lines up tall bamboos. She picked all that there were, and wondered whether they were better than Violet Faversham's. She carried them back to the house, stooping a little as she walked, for she was tired, as she so often was nowadays. All her attention was concentrated on her present task, for so she had trained herself to ward away unpleasant thoughts.

She looked at the roses; there were plenty of tight buds, but these she would leave to gather in the freshness of the morning. She kept her vases in the cloakroom cupboard, and now she went to fetch those she would need for her arrangements tomorrow, so that she could leave them ready in the porch beside the flowers. There was a wide, urn-shaped one for her mixed bowl; two small matching baskets for the pair class; an old, elaborate silver bowl for the roses. Somewhere there should be a plain white pottery one that was a perfect container for sweet peas. It was not in the cupboard. Surely it had not been broken? She had not used it lately in the house. Suddenly she remembered. It had been filled with hyacinth bulbs last winter, and she must have stored it in the cellar with the other bulb bowls, ready for next autumn's planting.

Mrs. Trent walked round the side of the house towards the cellar steps; she was light of foot, and wearing rubber-soled canvas shoes; Victor did not hear her on the stairs.

The cellar door was open, and after the evening sunlight it was dark inside. She screwed up her eyes and more by instinct than vision went over to the ledge where she knew the bowls to be. The figure that rose up from its seat on a pile of coke in the dimness took her entirely by surprise. She was too startled to scream; she shrank back, hands to her mouth, heart thumping, and it was not till he spoke that she recognised her own son.

XI

Nick was determined to be naughty tonight. He splashed the bathwater all round the room and drenched his mother; he would not co-operate in the putting on of his pyjamas, and kept getting two plump legs into one trouser-hole; he seized the toothpaste tube and squeezed a nasty white worm all round the basin and on to the floor. Finally he pulled Julia's hair and made her cry.

Susan, already over-wrought with the worry of her visit from the police and her subsequent fears, was short with him. She was eager to get both children tucked up in bed as soon as possible, and because of this wish, operations took even longer than usual. Nick spilled his mug of milk all down his front and had to be changed into a clean pair of pyjamas; Julia discovered a splinter in her hand, and was so lacking in courage that its extraction, very gently by Elizabeth, took three times as long as it need. Then she elected to brush her own hair, and got it into such a tangle that it took her mother and aunt ten minutes to restore order, each working on one side of her head.

Ever ready to snatch an opportunity, however, Julia said when this was going on, "Mummy, now you see how silly it is for me to have long hair, can't I have it short?"

Susan's temper snapped. "I don't care how you have your hair," she said crossly, tugging at the disputed locks. "You can have it off tomorrow as far as I'm concerned. Now into bed with you both, and don't let me hear another sound until breakfast time tomorrow."

Julia looked solemnly at her reflection in the mirror, and slowly a beam of delight stretched from ear to ear. She caught Elizabeth's eye gave her a large, elaborate wink.

"Come on, you heard what Mummy said. Into bed," said Elizabeth with a smile. She sped her niece on her way with a gentle spank, and glanced curiously at Susan, who seemed very jumpy this evening and in rather a bad temper. Her good humour was a by-word; it was almost unknown for Susan to be brusque and snappy. Perhaps she and Hugh had quarrelled, though that seemed hardly probable. More likely she was worrying about her mother's increasing pallor and fatigue, which was a genuine reason for concern.

There was further justification for this theory at dinner; Mrs. Trent's face was ashen; she could hardly speak coherently and she demanded a stiff whisky and soda, which was a most unusual request for her to make. Even the unobservant Brigadier asked her if she was well.

"I do feel a little tired," she admitted, realising her behaviour could hardly be called normal. "It must be the heat."

"You shouldn't have gone picking all those damned flowers after tea. Susan would have done it for you," said her husband.

"No, perhaps I shouldn't," she agreed with rare meekness.

Susan persuaded her to go and rest in the drawing-room after dinner, while Elizabeth and Hugh washed up, and her mother seized her arm to prevent her from joining them.

"Susan, I must speak to you, while they're busy," she said urgently. "We must get away from Daddy. Let's go into the garden."

"But are you sure you're all right? Hadn't you better sit down?" said the girl anxiously.

"No, no, I'm perfectly all right," said Mrs. Trent impatiently. "We must go quickly before the others follow us. Come on."

She moved out through the french window and Susan went after her, taking her arm to steady her.

It was a few minutes before her mother could find words. Then she said, "Susan, prepare yourself for a terrible shock. Victor was one of those men who escaped from prison and he's here."

Susan stared at her, speechless. "Here! But that's impossible!" she gasped at last.

"No it isn't. He's hiding in the cellar," said Mrs. Trent in a voice that shook.

Susan held her arm more firmly. "Now keep quite calm and tell me all about it," she said.

Mrs. Trent began, disjointedly. "It was because of the flower bowls. Daddy said I shouldn't have done them tonight and he was right. I'd left one in the cellar,—that white pottery one, you remember, that the blue hyacinths were in last year —I wanted it for the sweet peas, and I went down to fetch it, and there he was, sitting on the coke."

"But I don't understand," said Susan in bewilderment. "He wasn't there this morning when the police came."

"He said they'd been, but he didn't say you were with them! So you knew, Susan! Why didn't you tell me?"

"I didn't know he was here, and I didn't want to worry you," said Susan slowly. "I knew you'd have to hear in the end, but I thought it would be easier for you if we could keep it from you till he'd been caught again. Oh, how could he come here like this, upsetting us all again!" Her plump face looked tragic. "We must turn him in, of course. Who else knows he's here? And where was he when the police came?"

"He burrowed under the coke," said Mrs. Trent. Pride at his success in avoiding discovery struggled with proper dismay in her voice. "He didn't say anyone else knew he was here," she added.

"What about Elizabeth?" asked Susan.

"Well, she was in church this morning so she couldn't have

seen him then, and she was out walking this afternoon, and she's been with her children until now, I don't see how she could know. He got here during the night, he said," Mrs. Trent told her. "Oh, Susan, need we give him up? Poor Elizabeth, think how upset she would be, and I had hoped she would have a happy weekend with Richard, she gets so little to enjoy."

"With Richard? Do you mean—?" Susan's voice trailed away and she stared incredulously at her mother.

Mrs. Trent nodded. "I didn't mean to tell anyone, it's something I just guessed myself, but now this business makes a difference," she said soberly.

"Oh, what a mess!" Susan exclaimed. "Poor Elizabeth. And whatever happens to Victor it's hopeless because he's a parson."

Her mother nodded again. "So do let's allow them to enjoy tomorrow if we can," she pleaded. "I made Victor promise to leave during the night. I'll take him some food and some money; I suppose there isn't much chance that he'll get far, but if only he could get out of the country Elizabeth would be free, even though she couldn't marry Richard."

Some money; there is was again. Susan could not put Elizabeth's strange request out of her mind; however, if she did know about Victor's escape obviously she wanted to keep the news to herself, so it would be best not to interfere with her plans by speaking to her about it. Probably it was all a coincidence, for surely Victor would have told Mrs. Trent if he had been in touch with his wife.

"Very well, Mummy," said Susan at last. "I won't breathe a word, but all the same I'd like to give him a piece of my mind. I think you'd better take him the food and money, I won't offer to do it for you. I daren't trust myself not to flay him alive." She pressed her mother's arm. "Now, cheer up, Mummy, we've been through worse than this. Even if they do catch him there won't be another trial, we shan't have to face that again."

"No," Mrs. Trent smiled faintly, finding courage again. "I'm so glad I told you, Sue, I feel better already."

"What mischief are you two plotting?" asked Hugh, ambling over the lawn towards them.

"Oh, we're just deciding how we can best steal the sweet pea prize from under Lady Faversham's nose," said Susan. "Come along, Mummy, now you must show me your bottled raspberries."

She led Mrs. Trent firmly off towards the kitchen, which Elizabeth and Hugh had left supremely neat and orderly after finishing the washing-up.

"There, wasn't that a good bit of manoeuvring?" she said smugly. "Now we can pack up some food, and I'll see that the coast's clear while you take it down to Victor. See what good conspirators we'd be!"

Her mother smiled in spite of herself, for Susan had an enviable gift of seeming to find humour in any situation, however grim. She went into the larder and looked vaguely round. Two skeletonic chickens sat side by side beneath a wire mesh cover. She lifted this off, and said in a puzzled voice, "I thought there were some chicken legs left, they would have done nicely."

"Yes, there were three left," Susan agreed, coming to inspect the carcases. "Where can they have gone? I hope the children haven't swiped them. But I don't think they could have, they'd have left the bones lying about and we'd have seen them. And Rusty wouldn't be able to reach up here."

"Oh, well, never mind," said Mrs. Trent. "There's plenty of the joint left, we'll make some sandwiches with that."

Susan got the bread board out and began to butter and cut thick slices of bread, while her mother inexpertly carved large pieces from the leg of lamb. They had just finished when Elizabeth appeared.

"What are you doing?" she asked. She was so keyed up herself that she did not notice Susan's guilty blush or Mrs. Trent's startled movement.

Susan had been wrapping the sandwiches in greaseproof paper. As Elizabeth entered the room she bundled them hastily into the table drawer. "We were planning how to feed the five thousand tomorrow," she said lightly. "Mummy's got a huge tin of ham and one of tongue, and there's an enormous salmon in the frig. We must make some fruit salad and things in the morning. We shall be very busy."

"Yes, we shall," agreed Elizabeth eagerly. The false note in their voices struck both girls simultaneously, and they glanced suspiciously at each other for a moment. Then Susan laughed. "Come along, Elizabeth," she said. "Let's challenge Daddy and Hugh to a game of Canasta. Mummy's tired and she's going to bed."

XII

By eleven o'clock the house was quiet. Mrs. Trent, duly excused from the card game, was thought to have been in bed long since, resting before the heavy day tomorrow. The others had played hilariously until after ten o'clock, when with large yawns they had followed her.

In front of the mirror, Susan sat creaming her face, and meditating on whether or not to confide in Hugh, for much as she longed for the comfort of doing so, the picture had altered since tea-time. Large, solid and supremely sensible, he plodded to and fro, shedding garments and folding each one neatly before he laid it on a chair for the night. Just as she was drawing breath to speak, he said, " Funny, all those policemen about, did you notice? Cars whizzed up and down the lane all day. Must have an escaped loony or something in the district."

Susan said carefully, " Don't you remember, Daddy said last night two prisoners had escaped from Moorhurst."

" Oh, so he did," Hugh remembered. Then he added indifferently, " Well, they'll soon be back again. More fools they, they've no hope of escaping with all the police in the country on their trail. I suppose they must have come in this direction." He turned his socks tidily inside out ready to put on again. " Moorhurst; that's where Victor is, isn't it?"

Susan nodded. Surely by her face Hugh would guess, she thought, feeling that in spite of the dabs of cream on her round cheeks she looked like a tragedy queen. But now Hugh, having disposed methodically of his own clothing was collecting her shoes and putting them neatly side by side.

"Well, if he's one of them, he wouldn't be so silly as to come here," he said with assurance. "Dash it, one would have to give him up at once. By the way, is your mother all right, Sue? I thought she looked pretty grim at dinner."

The moment for confidence was over. Susan heard herself calmly repeating Mrs. Trent's theory that she had overdone things in the heat.

Much later, when Susan in spite of all her tension lay sleeping, Hugh was still awake, and found himself thinking along curious lines. During the day it had slowly dawned upon his not over-perceptive mind that family behaviour was not quite as usual. Elizabeth had looked as white as a ghost, and though charming as ever had seemed to join in conversation with only half of her attention; then this afternoon she had disappeared for ages, when normally she spent every spare moment playing with Nick and Julia. Susan had been touchy and irritable, and looked tired tonight, which was rare for her since she was blessed with singularly robust health; at tea-time her humour had been forced. Mrs. Trent in particular had looked ill this evening. Only the Brigadier remained unchanged. Perhaps they had all heard about the escaped prisoners, and the news had upset them, as well it might, but if so it was odd that Susan at least had not mentioned it to him earlier. It was curious that so many patrols had driven up the lane. Could it be possible that Victor was one of the men at large? Hugh's opinion of his brother-in-law was not high, but surely even he would not be so stupid? He lay, unable to sleep, wrestling with these problems.

Elizabeth too was wakeful. She felt desperately tired, but it would not do to drop off to sleep. She watched the luminous hands of her clock moving round at a snail's pace. So much seemed to have happened since Victor appeared at her window that it was hard to realise that only twenty-four hours had passed. The house was still, but the silence seemed full of foreboding. Victor would be wondering when she was coming. At last she decided everyone must be asleep, and she got up.

She opened her door very quietly, and went along the passage, using a torch so that she need not risk the clicking of the light switches. She went softly down the back staircase, out through the kitchen door and round to the cellar.

Victor jumped up when he saw the beam of her torch approaching. "Thank goodness you're here, I thought you were never coming," he said.

"I had to wait till everyone was asleep," she replied. She shone her light upon him. "Goodness, you're black! What have you been doing?" she exclaimed.

"The police came here this morning while you were at church," he said, again suppressing Susan's part in the adventure. "Luckily I heard them; I unlocked the door because they'd only have broken it down if the key wasn't there. I hid under the coke."

"Oh, Victor, how awful!" cried Elizabeth. Because he did not mention her, she assumed Susan must have been playing with Nick down by the brook, and so remained ignorant of what had happened. She thought of the agony of suspense he must have been in while the police peered into his retreat.

"Well, your luck was in," she said briefly. "Now we must clean you up somehow, you'll never escape notice like that." She looked at him in perplexity, and suddenly began to laugh. "To think I was going to bring you a small bowl of water," she said. "That wouldn't have gone far." She heard her own voice break a little, and pulled herself together.

"You'll have to have a bath," she decided at last. "It's a risk we must take. We'll use the small bathroom at the end of the house, away from all the bedrooms, and we'll just have to hope no one hears." She thought for a minute. "I'll go and get it ready, then if anyone wakes I can pretend it's for me. Watch for my torch to shine out of the landing window; that will mean it's safe for you to come in. You'd better leave your trousers and coat in the kitchen or there will be a trail of dust all through the house. I'll see if I can find you some other clothes."

She vanished into the darkness, and Victor waited outside the cellar door, thankful for once to be told what to do. Ten minutes later he saw the pale gleam of the torch shining from the house and he quickly went inside. It was strange to return so secretly in the night, to this familiar place.

The bath was a luxury, and he revelled in it. He felt cleaner than for years when, shaved, and with his cropped head washed, he got out of the now black water. Elizabeth appeared with the Vim and began to remove the tidal mark he left, and told him that everything was still quiet.

Then, wearing only his prison underclothes, Victor went with her down to the kitchen where she had already started to cook him a meal.

XIII

Hugh, at last on the fringe of sleep, suddenly was alert, roused by a faint sound from far away in the house. He listened hard, the familiar sense of emergency he had known during the war coming back to him; but the noise was not repeated and gradually he lapsed back again into slumber. Some time later another sound penetrated his consciousness; it was a gurgling noise like bath water running away. How odd of someone to want a bath at this hour. He grunted and rolled over. But when for the third time Hugh was disturbed, he sat up.

XIV

As became a Sunday evening, the bar at the Rose and Crown was well-filled, with the holiday bringing in a few extra customers to add to the usual locals, but though busy it was yet quiet and orderly. Mr. Brown of the Emporium consumed his weekly indulgence and chatted with Mr. Meaker; two or three heated cyclists called in to cool themselves; and during the evening all Bert Higgs' regulars dropped in.

Ivy, wearing a tight black satin dress which left little to the imagination though it was more sober than most of her outfits, officiated behind the bar. She was hoping that Alan would have changed his duty so that he could come and see her after all, and every time the door opened she looked swiftly up to see who was coming in; but each time she was disappointed. Everyone was astonished when P.C. Hopkins walked self-consciously inside and laid his helmet down upon the counter.

"Hey, mind out, you'll get it wet if you leave it there," said Ivy, picking it up and mopping at the circles of spilt beer that ringed the counter top. "Well, and what can I get for you?" she asked in solicitous tones.

The policeman felt extremely uncomfortable, knowing very well that everyone was slyly commenting on his unusual presence in the inn, with many smiles and chuckles.

"Er, um, a glass of lemonade, please, my dear," he said loudly in a patronising way, determined to let everyone know that he had not fallen for the demon drink.

With elaborate ceremony Ivy poured out a bottle of lemonade, and P.C. Hopkins gingerly picked it up. He went over to the table where Mr. Brown was sitting. "Mind if I sit here?" he asked in what he hoped was a genial voice, and lowered himself into a chair. "Cheerio," he cried gaily, and took a large swig of his innocuous drink. Its powerful fizz caught him unawares and shamed him before them all, but he rallied.

"How's business?" he asked jovially. "Anything unusual happened over the weekend?"

"Certainly not." Mr. Brown looked pained. "Unusual things don't happen in my shop," he said coldly, eyeing the policeman with dislike. Whatever was he up to, barging in like this and interrupting a most interesting conversation about a system for next season's pools. But P.C. Hopkins, having plucked up the courage to enter this den of iniquity, was not to be lightly put off.

"Not seen any strangers about? Did no one unusual come in to the shop?" he persisted.

"No one at all," said Mr. Brown crossly, "excepting young Mrs. Trent wanting to cash a cheque this afternoon. Pretty cool on a Sunday afternoon."

Hopkins pricked up his ears.

"Cheek, I call it," went on Mr. Brown grumblingly. "Putting folks to trouble like that. Still, I must say she's a real nice lady and said she was sorry, not like some people who come poking their noses in where they're not wanted." He glowered meaningly at the policeman.

Ivy overheard their conversation. Round-eyed with amazement she was just opening her mouth to speak when her father dug her in the ribs.

"Not a word, my girl," he muttered. "Mrs. Trent's affairs are nothing to do with P.C. Hopkins."

But like his daughter, Bert Higgs was puzzled and intrigued.

XV

Richard sat up late, trying to read, but anxiously going over the events of the day. The Priory was too far away from the Vicarage for him to see its lights, and he longed to know what was happening there. He wondered whether Victor was far away by now, and would have gone to the church to see whether he had taken the money, if it had not meant being away from the telephone; it would be dreadful if Elizabeth called for help and he was not there.

But at midnight all was still; it was a lovely night, warm and clear, and promised well for tomorrow's weather. The Trents must all have gone to bed by this late hour; for him to stay up any longer would serve no useful purpose. Richard closed his book and turned the light out. Then he limped slowly and quietly up the stairs, went softly past Mrs. Maggs door pausing for a moment to listen to her gusty snores, and so into his own bedroom.

But it was almost dawn before he slept.

XVI

"You must have a good meal, Victor, to last you for as long as possible, and I'll make you some sandwiches to take with you," said Elizabeth. She went in to the larder to fetch what she needed, and Victor made no effort to tell her about the food his mother had already given him, for he knew very well how angry she would be if she realised Mrs. Trent had seen him. He sat on a kitchen chair, still dressed in his underclothes and one of his father's shirts that Elizabeth had found in the airing cupboard.

It was odd to be sitting here in the middle of the night: this was the home he had known ever since he was a tiny boy; every stick and stone of it was familiar to him, but this time he came to it like the thief that he was, scarcely daring to speak in case his presence was discovered. He was a little frightened of the amount of deception he had practised on his family today, but they could sort it out between them when he had gone; he was uncertain of how much help he would have from Elizabeth if she knew what he had been doing. He watched her now as she dished up a steaming plate full of bacon and chips, with three fried eggs. It smelled delicious and after his diet of sandwiches Victor's mouth watered. He practically fell upon it, shovelling it in to his mouth in huge amounts with no pretence at politeness. He was vaguely aware, beyond the horizon of his plate, that Elizabeth was moving quietly round, collecting the things she had used and putting them on the draining board. She was still lovely, though she looked strained and pale, with an apron neatly tied over her crisp blue and white dressing-gown. Victor glanced at her between mouthfuls; she'll soon be rid of me, he thought, I simply must succeed this time. He longed to be on his way again, yet he was reluctant to leave the comparative safety he was in and fend for himself.

" Quite like old times, seeing you at the sink, Elizabeth," he said in an effort to break the silence that seemed suddenly frightening.

" For goodness' sake whisper; we don't want to wake everyone up," she said.

" Do they know I've got out?" he asked.

She shook her head. " No, thank heaven," she said, " and they mustn't either, till you're well away from here. It puzzles me why the police didn't speak to Susan this morning, though thank goodness they didn't. I suppose she was down the garden and they thought we were all out. But I always imagined the first thing they did was to question the family of an escaped man. It will be a terrible shock for them when they do hear."

" Have you got the cash?" asked Victor.

She nodded. "And what a job it was," she said. "Susan thought I was mad wanting to borrow money on a Sunday, and I had quite a struggle cashing cheques in the village. I only hope you do get away after all this, Victor."

" I will, never you fear," he said confidently.

" Don't be too cocky," she warned, taking his empty plate away and putting a large slice of fruit cake in front of him. " The police are swarming all over the roads. As they've been here it proves they're watching for you. Probably they've traced you to the district. What do you intend to do?"

Victor, his mouth full of crumbly cake and currants, answered indistinctly. " I shall stick to the fields, and go round the hill towards Haverstoke, along the river. There's plenty of cover along the banks. Then I'll hop on a train. You're right that I'll have a better chance of not being noticed if I get amongst the holiday crowds."

"You must leave before dawn," said Elizabeth. " It will be pandemonium here tomorrow with everyone getting ready for the Flower Show, and your mother has a large party for lunch. You must be well away by then."

Victor said, " I'll leave in a couple of hours, and lie up in the fields for a bit. It'll look fishy if I arrive in Haverstoke too early."

" Yes." Elizabeth was busy cutting bread and butter. " Well, you don't deserve to get away but after all this I hope you do. I'll be wishing you luck," she said, and she softened the harshness of her manner by smiling at him. " Now finish that cake up quickly. The sooner you're out of the house the better. It only needs Nick to have a nightmare and wake everyone up for the whole family to troop down here and find you."

" Tell me about them," said Victor. " How are the kids?"

" Well, Julia's mad to have her plaits cut and Susan can't make her mind up about it," said Elizabeth. " Nick's a pet,

so plump and cuddly." She went on talking softly while he
drank the mug of coffee she had given him, only pausing to
fetch the remains of the joint from the larder.

"There's not much left of this," she said. "I didn't think
we'd made such a big hole in it at lunch. Oh, well, you may
as well finish it. I'll have to make poor Rusty take the blame
if it's missed." She sliced it up neatly and took the bone back
to the larder. The door fell to with a thud behind her and she
jumped at the sudden noise. They both waited motionless for
a moment, but there was no other sound, and Elizabeth
resumed her task of bundling up the sandwiches. She filled a
flask with steaming hot cocoa.

"This is very nourishing," she said. "You don't want to
stop for food unless you must. They'll be looking out for you
in cafés. I'll go upstairs in a minute and see what clothes I
can find."

Victor saw with satisfaction the large pile of provisions she
had got for him. Combined with what his mother had prepared there was enough for several days.

Elizabeth took his mug and began to wash it up with the
plates he had used. The noise of the water in the sink drowned
the small sound of Hugh's approach along the passage. They
were both taken completely by surprise when he opened the
door.

Elizabeth was the first to find her tongue.

"Hugh, don't say anything for a minute," she begged, while
Victor, ridiculous in shirt and underpants, shrank into a
corner.

Hugh was a most law-abiding citizen; what hope was there
that he would keep silent? He advanced now, slowly, into the
room, a poker in his hand, followed by Rusty, that ferocious
watch-dog, with genially wagging tail.

"Well," he said at last, "you'd better do the explaining,
Elizabeth," and. to his brother-in-law, "the less I hear from
you the better."

Looking round, he saw the evidence of Victor's meal, the
packet of food and the thermos flask.

"Oh, Hugh, it's obvious, surely," said Elizabeth, near to

tears. All her work and worry seemed now to be in vain. "Victor escaped and came here. He hid in the cellar. I was helping him, because I didn't want Mother to know. There wouldn't be such a fuss if he was caught somewhere else. It would kill her to have him found here."

Hugh nodded slowly, thinking hard. He had not known quite what he expected to find when he saw the beam of light beneath the kitchen door. In spite of his suspicions he had not really anticipated that his brother-in-law would be here so soon.

"Haven't you got any clothes?" he asked Victor, eyeing him with dislike.

"He got filthy in the cellar, amongst the coke," Elizabeth interpolated swiftly, deciding to suppress the visit from the police.

Hugh said, "You'll never get away. The police are round the place like bees round a hive, though I hadn't realised you were the reason."

"I can go over the fields," said Victor sulkily. He watched Hugh warily, sensing his antagonism, for there had never been any love lost between the two.

"Hugh, go back to bed," said Elizabeth, pulling herself together. "Pretend you never heard a thing; then you need know nothing about it whatever happens."

Hugh waved a hand impatiently. "That's not what's worrying me," he said. "Victor, didn't you think of all the trouble you'd cause by doing this? Haven't you put your family through enough shame without adding to it? What hope have you got of getting right away? None at all. It's a wonder your parents don't already know of your escape; certainly they will in a day or two. Why couldn't you take your punishment like a man?" He glared at Victor, who answered in a surly voice.

"If I can only get to the coast, I'll jump a ship. Then none of you will be bothered with me any more."

Elizabeth explained, "He's got some friend watching out for him at Hull. Hugh, don't ring the police. Let him go."

Hugh looked at her consideringly. "Has it occurred to you,

Elizabeth, that if he's found here you'll be in a nasty spot yourself? For helping him, I mean."

"Wives can't give evidence against their husbands," she said.

"But I imagine you might be prosecuted for sheltering him." Large and solid, arrayed in a bright yellow Paisley dressing-gown, Hugh looked like British Justice personified. He admired Elizabeth, though what she had seen in Victor he never knew, for he'd always been one of those smooth chaps. But she'd certainly paid dearly for her misguided choice and deserved no further trouble. He saw her watching him, white and tense, and made up his mind.

"I've got a jacket and a pair of trousers upstairs you can have," he said. "I'll fetch them. But see that you're gone by five o'clock. If you're still here then I'll report you at once." He turned and left the room, followed by Rusty.

"Phew," Victor whistled, mopping his face. "I thought we'd had it that time. Wouldn't have believed old Hugh'd have it in him."

Elizabeth made no comment. She was much too shaken. She turned to finish tidying away the plates and dishes.

"I'll go and find a case for you to carry the sandwiches in," she said.

"Wait till Hugh comes back. Don't leave me alone," Victor implored her, seizing her arm.

She saw how Hugh's appearance had unnerved him, and freed herself.

"Pull yourself together, Victor," she said briskly. "You'll never get away unless you find your courage."

He had the grace to look ashamed. "I'm jolly grateful for what you've done," he muttered sheepishly.

"Well, don't waste it all then, by losing your nerve," she answered briefly.

In a few minutes Hugh returned with a tweed jacket and a pair of grey flannel trousers.

"Here, get into these," he said. "They'll be a bit big but it can't be helped."

Victor put them on quickly. He gathered the surplus

material round his waist into a belt. The fit left much to be desired, for Hugh could no longer be called slim.

"Well, beggars can't be choosers," said Victor philosophically, beginning to recover his confidence now that he was clothed.

"Here's some money and a bar of chocolate," said Hugh gruffly. Dash it, the fellow was his brother-in-law, after all.

"I must find a bag to put these sandwiches in, and the flask," said Elizabeth. "Will you keep watch, Hugh? I'll be quick."

She went upstairs and found an old Gladstone bag of the brigadier's in the box room. It looked a highly respectable piece of luggage and would lend tone to Victor's appearance.

Hugh stood silently, a disapproving sentry, while she packed it.

"Now you must go, Victor," she said. "Goodbye, and good luck." She hesitated for a moment, then she kissed him lightly on the cheek.

Hugh coughed. "Er, take care, Victor," was all he could manage. It was too much to expect good fortune to be on the side against the law. They opened the kitchen door and let the fugitive out into the night. Neither watched to see whether he returned to his cellar or went at once upon his way, for it was better not to know.

Now Hugh produced a flask from his dressing-gown pocket.

"Here, Elizabeth, you look as if you could do with some of this," he said abruptly. "Drop of brandy to pull you together."

Elizabeth began to laugh, very quietly, and her laughter was mixed up with tears. "Oh, Hugh, you have been splendid," she said, fighting to regain control. "You are a comfort, no wonder Susan is so happy."

Hugh poured a generous tot of brandy into a glass and handed it to her. "Drink it up," he said in some embarrassment. "Always find it helps in a crisis."

Women, he thought, resignedly; what fantastic creatures, one minute as cool as cucumbers, as though helping criminals was an every day matter, and the next second weeping helplessly like children. He would never learn to understand the sex.

XVIII

Late on Sunday night, under cover of darkness, the old grey bus and the ramshackle lorry trundled into Bramsbourne from the roadside pitch where it had rested for the day. The evening at Dimbleton had been surprisingly successful; fired with the holiday spirit the little place had held fiesta, and Dad was a very happy man when he counted his takings.

It was annoying to be stopped by the police as they chugged noisily down the road; still more annoying to have the van searched from top to bottom. The children were all excited, hopping about and getting in the way of the policeman; dirty-faced and lively, they chattered like monkeys.

" Seen any one suspicious about? Picked anyone up?" asked the sergeant curtly. He had no patience with vagabonds.

" Why, whatever's up?" Mum prevaricated.

" Couple of convicts escaped from Moorhurst," answered the sergeant. " Well, seen anyone?" He was bored; it was time he went off duty, but his relief was late. He waited impatiently.

Mum and Dad exchanged a look. Their policy was always to keep on the right side of the police, yet he'd seemed such a nice young fellow and ever so handy with a screwdriver; it seemed a shame to give him up. But they'd never thought that he'd escaped; they'd assumed he'd just been let out. Very reluctantly Dad said, " We picked a bloke up outside Gloucester on Friday."

" Recognise him?" Instantly the sergeant, reinvigorated, held a sheaf of photographs under his nose. Dad looked slowly through them; then he picked out one.

" That's him," he said. " We dropped him the other side of Dimbleton on Saturday afternoon."

" He'll be miles away by now. I expect. Just my luck," said the sergeant, who longed for promotion.

Dad said, " He told me he was going to—" and then changed his mind. He'd told them where he'd left the chap, now let them get on with it themselves. "Going to press on hard," he ended.

The sergeant wasted no more time. He scrambled down from the lorry and began giving instructions to his subordinates.

Dad started the engine up again and drove on, hoping that Victor had not decided to accept his offer of another lift an Tuesday.

XIX

Inspector Howard lay peacefully sleeping beside his wife Mary in their large double-bed at The Nook. His unsolved problems were abandoned for the moment; the annoyance of his Superintendent at his failure so far to recapture Victor Trent was forgotten. He snored gently; in due time the fugitive would be found.

Presently the shrilling of the telephone awoke him. He blinked and sat up, reaching for the receiver automatically.

"Howard here. Yes. What? Speak up, man, speak up. Oh, right, good. Double all watches on roads and inform neighbouring forces," he said, instantly alert. "He'll be miles away by now but we must leave nothing to chance. Got it? Right, I'll be down first thing in the morning."

He hung up and submerged himself again in the bedclothes. Mary had scarcely stirred, accustomed to his disturbed nights. Inspector Howard closed his eyes and relaxed. Well trained and efficient in every sphere, he was immediately asleep again.

At five o'clock he woke up suddenly.

"The cellar! I knew there was something funny about that cellar!" he cried aloud. "There were bits of coke all over the floor, and that dust in the air! The coke must have been disturbed to make a dust like that."

He leaped out of bed and began rapidly to dress.

PART FOUR

MONDAY

I

B ILLY B ROWN, son of Mr. Brown of the Bramsbourne Emporium, daily performed the duties of paper-boy in the village on his way to school, a fact that was tolerantly overlooked by P.C. Hopkins since he depended upon Billy to deliver his own newspaper. He collected the papers at Bramsbourne Halt, where they were brought by an early train from Haverstoke, and then bicycled round the village taking them to all the houses and cottages. In this way Bramsbourne was efficiently served, and those who breakfasted late could enjoy the latest news with their toast and marmalade.

On Bank Holiday Monday Billy, who had inherited some of his father's lugubrious nature, felt himself a martyr to be working while the rest of the world sat at ease. The fact that the railwaymen were also on duty did nothing to stop him feeling ill-used, and he spared no thought for the well-being of his customers.

"Serve them right if they all had to walk and fetch their own," he muttered, as he pedalled along on his stream-lined three-speed roadster. He went from house to house, poking the rolled up papers into gateposts and letter-boxes, exerting himself to the minimum, not troubling to glance at the headlines, and undisturbed to discover that he had delivered Miss Finch's *Daily Shout* at the vicarage by mistake. It did not occur to him to put right his error; he simply shoved Richard's *Times* into Miss Finch's door-latch instead.

On he went: to the Rose and Crown; to the Hall where the Favershams lived; to the Priory; and to all the humbler dwellings; a wheeled Mercury bringing communication from the world beyond Bramsbourne, where excitement and thrills happened every day to fill the pages with titillating news.

Bert Higgs sat in his shirt sleeves having a quick glance through his own paper to make sure he missed no spectacular murder before he went down to the Big Meadow.

"Phew," he whistled sharply, as he scanned the middle page.

"What is it, Dad?" asked Ivy. Her mood today was uncertain; she had not decided whether to feel tragic, as she had done yesterday, or whether to resume her normal sublime indifference to everything unconnected with herself; so whilst she made up her mind she thought it worth enquiring what was so startling. Perhaps another lurid Hollywood divorce was pending.

"Remember those two convicts who escaped?" Bert said. "Well, what do you think? One of them was young Trent!"

"No!" Ivy stared, round-eyed, impressed at last. "Well, I never! Have they caught him yet?"

Bert was reading on. "No, not yet," he said. "Look, here's his photo. Not very good though, is it?"

Ivy leaned over his shoulder to inspect the picture.

"No, I suppose it isn't," she agreed. "Though p'raps he looks a bit different after two years in jug. My, what a bit of excitement!"

Bert nodded. "It'll upset them all at the Priory," he said. "I don't expect they'll come to the Show now."

"Oh, won't they?" Ivy looked crestfallen, remembering how she had persuaded Elizabeth to agree to introduce her to Harley Darrell.

"It says here the police think he may have been making in the direction of his home," Bert said.

"P'raps that's why old Hopkins came in last night," suggested Ivy. "He may have thought we'd got him hiding under the counter."

Bert laughed. "Well, I expect he'll have to keep a lookout," he said. "He might get himself promoted if he was the one to find him."

"Well," said Ivy. "Would you believe it, an escaped convict in Bramsbourne! I hope I don't meet him, I shouldn't half scream."

"He won't hurt you, my girl, if you do meet him," said her father. "He isn't that sort of convict. And anyway, it doesn't say he's here, only that he may be coming. The police'll collar him if he comes anywhere near, you mark my words."

"And to think she was in here only yesterday," marvelled Ivy, off on another tack and remembering Elizabeth. "Little did she know he was fleeing to her side!" Her imagination was caught, as would Miss Finch's have been if Billy Brown's inefficiency had not deprived her of her morning scandals.

"I shouldn't think young Mrs. Trent would be at all pleased to see him if he did turn up," said Bert realistically. He got up, and folded the newspaper again. "Well, I must be getting on, Ivy. It's time to go and meet the vicar. Mind you have dinner ready in good time."

The Favershams at the Hall subscribed to a picture paper as well as to *The Times*. They saw the photograph of Victor almost as early as Bert.

"Oh, poor Marjorie Trent," exclaimed Lady Faversham, looking through her pink-framed spectacles at the paragraph. "What a dreadful thing to happen!"

"Damned young idiot," growled Lord Faversham. "He'll never get away with it. What a stupid thing to do." He remembered his conversation with his old friend last night and groaned inwardly as he realised what this fresh blow would mean to the brigadier.

"And this weekend, of all times! Whatever will they do?" wondered Lady Faversham. She took off her glasses, for even in front of her husband she would not from vanity wear them unless she must. Now she peered myopically at him over the long dining table.

"Should I telephone and offer to have the luncheon here?" she debated. "What a bother that will be, for I've given the servants the day off thinking we'd be out." Alone in the district, Lady Faversham controlled something approaching a pre-war domestic staff. Everyone marvelled at her skill, and shuddered when they tried to calculate what it must cost. But the Favershams had no heir, and so no reason for trying to conserve their capital.

" But perhaps they don't know about it?" she went on, still thinking aloud.

" Sure to; the police must have been there," grunted Lord Faversham. He did not like conversation at breakfast, especially of such a nature, for it was too early in the day to cope with emotion.

" Well, the least I can do is to offer some sort of sympathy," decided Lady Faversham, rising from the table. She was still slim, and very elegant. With her blued hair and painted finger-nails she was typical of the readers of Elizabeth's magazine.

At the vicarage, Nanny Maggs came into Richard's study carrying the paper, as she did every day, but on this occasion wearing an expression of great disgust.

" Look what that Billy Brown has had the nerve to deliver here," she expostulated, holding out Miss Finch's *Daily Shout*. " Whatever does he think we are? Mind you tell him off, Master Dick, when you see him."

Richard smiled. " He's got the holiday spirit, I expect," he said tolerantly. " Never mind, I'll be too busy today to have more than a quick glance at any paper. You settle down to it, Maggie, you'll enjoy it."

" Bah !" said Mrs. Maggs in disapproval. " Well, it's not fit for you to see, that's certain. She folded it up, set her mouth in a prim line, and marched from the room. Three minutes later she reappeared.

" I just happened to glance inside this," she said with some diffidence, holding out the offending newspaper at arm's length as though it was full of elderly fish. " I think you should see it, Master Dick."

She handed it to him, folded to display the picture of Victor enlarged to three times the size of the one in Lord Faversham's less sensational paper

Richard looked at it in silence. His first thought was that it was a poor likeness. Then he took in the startling black headlines above it and the melodramatic wording of the story, and was appalled.

"As if there isn't enough misfortune without the papers getting hold of it," he said at last. "But I suppose they think it's their duty." He sighed. "Oh, Maggie, what do we do now?"

He looked very tired, and the old woman watched him anxiously.

"That poor young lady; and Mrs. Trent," she said.

Richard nodded slowly. The news would be all round the village by now. It was to be hoped that Victor was well away by this time, *en route* for the coast.

"I'll telephone," he said. "Perhaps I shall have to go round there. Bert Higgs will have to manage without me." He got up from his armchair and, dragging his leg, went stiffly over to his desk where the telephone stood. Mrs. Maggs watched him, shaking her head. "Tch, tch," she clicked her tongue, and went back to her kitchen, for even in crises the work must be done.

There was a flicker of interest at Alan Blake's R.A.F. station in the fact of Victor's escape, because his home was so near; the main opinion was that he was a silly fool to try and get away with it, mingled with reluctant admiration of his success to date.

"Better watch out if you're going to Bramsbourne to see that girl of yours," one young man suggested to Alan. "You might meet him in a lane and get your bike pinched."

Sunk in gloom, Alan did not answer; he was still trying to find a way to impress Ivy.

II

Harley Darrell, the well-known film star, woke in the elegant bedroom of his Mayfair flat at half past eight on Monday morning. Film stars are popularly supposed to lie between satin sheets, but Harley's, though palest green, were merely of fine linen. His valet set down the early morning tea tray beside the great man, and went to draw back the curtains.

Hot dusty air streamed in through the open windows from the London street outside. By week-ending in Town, Harley had flouted convention, but between one " Personal Appearance " on Saturday and another at Bramsbourne today he had felt the need of a quiet Sunday away from house parties and fans.

He sipped his tea and thought with gloom of the day ahead. What he would really like to do would be to lounge in old grey flannels and without a tie in some peaceful country place, unknown, unrecognised and unmobbed. How hopeless to find such a spot on a fine Bank Holiday in England. Instead, he must dress up in as glamorous array as possible, drive a hundred miles along crowded roads, and then be gracious, charming, and convey an impression of eternal youth and romance, to a considerable cross-section of humanity. He sighed; he no longer found it easy to live as his admirers expected.

Sounds from the bathroom next door indicated that his admirable manservant was preparing his bath. Harley Darrell, who had strangely enough been born plain John Smith, got out of bed; in an aroma of bath salts and toilet water he began the daily ritual of transforming himself from a middle-aged man with a thickening figure into a svelte Romeo.

Breakfast was ready when he had bathed and shaved; half a grapefruit, some coffee and thin toast was all his increasing waistline would permit. Harley sighed as he toyed with this feast, thinking nostalgically of bacon and eggs, and even kidneys and mushrooms. It really was a wearying business apeing Peter Pan. He wondered idly how much longer he would last before he was forced to accept the limits of his years. The thousands of his admirers would never let him slide gently into playing elderly parts; he longed for the strength of mind to abandon the struggle and buy a pub in the country for his retirement. Whenever he mentioned the subject to his studio and agent, they shuddered in horror, for to them he was a gold mine in these hazardous times, and they would not contemplate the idea. So he must diet, cream his face, and engage in every artifice to deceive the penetrating eye of the camera.

Dressing was a considerable operation. All his outfits were carefully planned with harmoniously toning shirts and ties; he had over fifty pairs of shoes from which to choose. But under all this splendour, beneath his silk vest, it was necessary to fasten a curious garment around his thickening middle—it wasn't a corset, oh dear me no, nothing as shaming as that—but it did do a little something to control that tell-tale bulge.

At last he was ready to brush his hair; thank goodness he still had plenty of that. His servant, watching him critically in the mirror with his head on one side, said, " We should have touched it up a bit yesterday, sir. Them ends are beginning to show again."

Harley peered more closely at his reflection. It was true; grey wisps were showing through the rich chestnut of his wavy hair.

" Well, it'll have to do," he said. " There isn't time now, if I'm to be in Bramsbourne for lunch. Anything special to remember today, Thompson?"

His valet, besides seeing that he was suitably groomed for every occasion, also acted as chauffeur, secretary and unofficial adviser.

" I don't think so, sir," he said. " Lunch with Brigadier and Mrs. Trent, easy names, them are. Oh, there was that letter we had on Saturday from the young girl wanting you to take her to Hollywood."

" Oh, that; yes, I remember," sighed the film star. " Silly young thing, I suppose I'm bound to meet her. I'll give her a fatherly talk, eh?"

He stood up and surveyed himself in the long mirror that was placed near a window in the luxurious room. Immaculate from the top of his tinted head to the tips of his gleaming shoes, erect, and concave at the waist, he was fully clothed in his public personality. He gave his tie a last tweak and practised once his devastating smile; then, followed by Thompson now disguised in his chauffeur's uniform, he descended splendidly in the lift to his waiting Bentley.

III

At six o'clock Susan heard a loud knocking at the front door and sat up in bed. The noise continued, so she jumped out and went to the window. Leaning perilously out, she could just see the corner of Inspector Howard's jacket as he stood in the porch pounding at the door. His gleaming police car was parked on the gravel sweep.

"This is it," she thought, and was surprised to find herself icily calm. "I'm coming," she shouted out of the window, and went to shake Hugh, for she could not cope single-handed with the discovery of Victor that must now come; he would not have left the Priory yet.

"Eh, what's that? What's up?" asked Hugh, blinking at his untimely awakening after so few hours of rest.

"There's a policeman outside, Hugh. You must wake up, he's come for Victor," said Susan urgently. "He's escaped," she remembered to explain.

Hugh was wide awake now. He recalled with horror the lawless events of the night.

"Oh, yes, I know all about it," he said grimly, once again getting out of bed and putting on his yellow dressing-gown.

"But you don't know he was in the cellar," cried Susan in astonishment.

"I do—there's no time to talk about it now, I'll tell you later," said Hugh. "You stay here and leave this to me. He'll be well away by now." He vanished, leaving Susan utterly astounded. A moment later she heard him drawing the bolt of the heavy front door; then came the murmur of voices. It could only be seconds before her father heard the unusual sounds in the house and came to investigate. She hovered between the window of her room and the door, ready to waylay him if he should come out on to the landing, in a last unreasoning effort to postpone enlightenment.

Down below Hugh was busy committing perjury. He looked the picture of outraged innocence, with his hair ruffled and his small moustache bristling indignantly. Attack being the best method of defence, he started before the inspector could speak, saying angrily, "What is the meaning of waking the household up at this unearthly hour?"

Inspector Howard was not to be deflected, however.

"I must inform you that your brother-in-law Victor Trent has escaped from prison and is suspected of being concealed in or about the premises," he rattled off. "I have here a warrant to search the house. I shall begin with the cellar."

Hugh now saw that a burly constable was already standing at the top of the cellar steps, and two other policemen were waiting near the car.

"By all means, search where you like," he said haughtily. "But I can assure you he's not here. We had no knowledge of his escape and this is the last place he would choose to hide in. His father would give him up at once, as should we all, naturally." He glared at Inspector Howard, with Major Bellamy's famous Look that had caused his troops to quail in the war.

The inspector without a word strode over to the steps and ran lightly down them. At the bottom he paused, for the fugitive might be armed; he banged on the door.

"Open up there, it's the police," he called sternly.

There was no sound.

"Open up, Trent, or I'll come and get you," he repeated.

Still no answer.

Inspector Howard opened the door quickly, and then jumped back, in case there should be a shot. Desperate men seized every wild chance of liberty.

Nothing happened. Cautiously the inspector went inside the cellar, followed by his sergeant and the burly constable, who had his truncheon at the ready.

All was quiet within. No dust clouds hung suspended in the air. The mounds of coke were just as they had always been. The pile of bulb bowls still stood upon their ledge.

"Get some shovels and turn all this coke over, sergeant," said Inspector Howard. "Bates, you help him. I'll search the house." He went up the steps again and spoke briefly to the other two policemen who had been poking hopefully about

in the bushes on the off chance that Victor might be lurking
there. Hugh, still, in his dressing-gown, was compelled to in-
dicate where they could find spades and shovels, but having
escorted them to the potting shed he stood grandly aside whilst
they helped themselves, too much on his dignity to hand the
tools over himself.

Without hurrying, he returned to lead Inspector Howard in
a second search of the house. They went round in silence;
at every door Hugh waited for the inspector to precede him
inside, then stood back in a bored way while he looked behind curtains, under sofas, and in every possible place.

Downstairs yielded no clue. Before they went up the stairs
Hugh said, " I must ask you to let me explain to Brigadier
and Mrs. Trent why you're here, and to my sister-in-law. They
have no idea that Victor has escaped, and I must prepare
them."

" Of course," said the inspector at once. Already he was
feeling a sense of anti-climax, for against all reasoning he
had still hoped to discover Victor skulking in the cellar, and
although a thorough search must be made it was unlikely that
he had spent all night buried under the coke.

Susan heard the heavy tread of her husband and his companion approaching down the passage, and she turned as
they entered the room.

" I'm afraid you must be ready for a shock, Susan," said
Hugh. " Victor has escaped from prison, and the inspector
thinks we're hiding him. I've told him it's ridiculous, but he
insists upon searching the house."

" But he did that yesterday and there was no one here,"
protested Susan. " I didn't tell my husband you'd been, Inspector, as you agreed there was no need to upset everybody.
Victor wasn't here yesterday, why should he be today?"

" We've reason to believe he was hiding in the cellar," said
the inspector. " I'm very sorry to disturb you all, Mrs. Bellamy, but I have my duty to do. May I search this room,
please."

" But of course. However, if you think he's in the cellar
why don't you look there?" she suggested.

"My men are down there, turning over the coke," stated the inspector briefly. He went methodically round the room, looking under the beds and in the wardrobe, while Susan watched.

"There's no one here, as you can see," she said. "I told you if he came I'd report it," she reminded him.

"In my belief he was hiding under the coke when I searched the cellar yesterday," said the inspector patiently "The atmosphere down there was full of dust as though it had been disturbed. It's possible he has now moved into the house, thinking himself to be safe. But he's not in here, so I'll leave you, Mrs. Bellamy, with apologies for troubling you."

"Must you go into the children's room?" asked Susan.

"Every room must be searched," said the inspector.

Susan raised her eyebrows at Hugh, who gave her an encouraging look. She pulled her dressing-gown around her more tightly and led the way into the night nursery.

Nicholas, completely naked, was dancing round the floor.

"Nick! Whatever are you doing? Where are your pyjamas??" cried Susan, running to pick him up.

"Me was hot so me bare," he said practically. "Me undid the cot by mine own self," he added with pride.

"Well, you're a very naughty little boy," Susan scolded. "Now back you get into bed and put your pyjamas on at once." She began bustling him into decency once more. "This policeman has lost something. He wants to look in here for it," she added, as the inspector peered into the cupboard.

Julia lay curled into a ball in bed. Only her bright eyes peeped out, watching.

"What have you lost?" she enquired. Her voice, coming from under the sheet, was muffled.

"Nothing very special, said Susan. "It isn't here anyway, is it, Inspector?"

"No, there's nothing here," said Inspector Howard.

"Now, Julia, you read to Nick till it's time to get up, and don't make a lot of noise," admonished Susan, before she followed the two men out of the room.

Elizabeth was on the landing. She had heard all the commotion and suddenly remembered that she had left Victor's dirty, discarded clothes down in the scullery. There had just been time to run and fetch them, and bundle them into a drawer amongst her own possessions, before the inspector and Hugh entered the house.

Once again Hugh went through his explanation for her benefit. Elizabeth gave a little cry, and gasped, " Oh, how could he?" in horrified tones, and her. acting perfectly satisfied the inspector. Hugh watched her with admiration; all sign of her small breakdown in the night had gone, and beyond a certain pallor she seemed as usual.

Her bedroom yielded no secrets. Now the dreaded moment when Victor's parents must be told could no longer be postponed. Susan said, " I'll tell them. Give me a few minutes, Inspector."

She slipped into her parents' room. Her mother was lying in bed, wide awake, eyes bright with anxiety.

" It's the police, Mummy," whispered Susan. " But it's all right, he's gone. I must wake Daddy."

The brigadier snored gently on. It took more than hammering on his own front door to rouse him from the depths of sleep. Susan shook him. " Wake up, Daddy," she said urgently. " You must wake up."

The snores ceased abruptly and the brigadier sat up.

" What's that? Eh? What's the matter, Susan? House on fire?"

" No, Daddy, no. Now you must keep calm," she said. She paused for a moment, and then plunged bravely. " Daddy, Victor has escaped and the police are here, looking for him. They want to search this room."

For a moment she thought her father would have a fit. His face went livid for an instant, and he seemed not to breathe. Then, just as suddenly, all the colour drained away from his cheeks and he looked a very old man.

" Then they must look," he said quietly. He got slowly out of bed and put on the thick brown Jaeger dressing-gown which he wore winter and summer alike. Then he put on his brown leather slippers and went to the door.

"You may come in, Inspector," he said heavily. "But there is no son of mine here."

IV

By seven o'clock Inspector Howard, a disappointed man, had gone away to make arrangements for more detailed enquiries in the villages around Bramsbourne; he had found no trace of Victor at the Priory. Two policemen were left behind to watch the house. One patrolled up and down outside the gate and the other strolled about near the brook; thus there was constant supervision of both sides and no one could approach from either direction without being seen.

Inside the house, the brigadier sat in his wing armchair, gazing into space. He had not spoken since his words to the inspector. Mrs. Trent watched him, wan, anxious, on the brink of collapse. Elizabeth and Hugh stood uneasily looking at them both and wondering what to say.

Then tension was broken by Susan coming into the drawing-room carrying a tray.

"I thought we could all do with a cup of tea," she announced cheerfully.

Like a tableau coming to life, everyone moved. Hugh bustled to bring forward a table, and Mrs. Trent said with a brave attempt at enthusiasm, "Oh, what a good idea, Sue." Even the brigadier seemed to return to them from wherever he had been with his thoughts, and turned his head to focus on the scene.

Susan poured out briskly, Hugh handed round the cups and Elizabeth passed the biscuit tin. Everyone drank, and as always the magic potion took swift effect. It became possible to face the situation.

"What shall we do?" said Mrs. Trent. "All those people are coming to lunch. We must put them off."

Now the brigadier spoke at last.

"We will do nothing of the sort," he said sternly, and a little colour began to return to his face. "Everything must go on just as we had arranged. No one need know of our trouble.

We will tell them the police are here to help with controlling the cars. There is no need to change our plans."

"But, Daddy," began Susan, about to mentioned the newspapers, who would surely today carry news of the escape. A warning glance from her mother stopped her.

"Of course, dear," said Mrs. Trent smoothly. "Victor can't be anywhere near here, and so it need make no difference at all." She smiled bravely and took a sip of tea. Somehow she had not been able to look at Elizabeth yet.

The brigadier got heavily to his feet. "Then that's settled," he said. "I'll finish my tea upstairs." He took a step towards the door; then he paused, and turned. "I'm sorry, Elizabeth, my dear," he said gravely. At the door he stopped again. "Thank God for you, anyway, Susan," he said. Then, very erect, he walked upstairs, carrying his cup and saucer in a hand as steady as a rock.

After he had gone the tension in the room relaxed still further, and now Mrs. Trent and Susan glanced at Elizabeth, for the shock to her must have been great. She seemed very calm, drinking her tea as though thinking of nothing in particular. Susan raised her eyebrows at her mother, as if to ask, shall we tell her, and imperceptibly Mrs. Trent shook her head. Simultaneously Hugh and Elizabeth exchanged a glance and a covert shake of the head. All thought, the less the others know the better.

Aloud Susan said, "The police came here yesterday while you were all in church. Of course there was nothing to find, but I didn't mention it as I didn't want to upset everyone."

"I understand, Sue," said Mrs. Trent gratefully. She glanced doubtfully at Elizabeth who still had not spoken.

"Father's right," she said now. "We mustn't let this make any difference, we'll go on as if it never happened."

Mrs. Trent said slowly, "There really is no new disgrace. We've no cause for further shame."

"Do you think Daddy's all right? Upstairs alone, I mean?" asked Susan anxiously.

"I think so," said Mrs. Trent. "He'd rather be by himself while he gets used to the idea. Perhaps it would be best not to talk about it in front of him unless he refers to it himself."

The others agreed.

" Well, there doesn't seem much point in going back to bed," said Susan. " We may as well get dressed and start the day. We've a lot to do before lunch so perhaps it's just as well to make an early beginning."

She began to collect the cups and saucers. Elizabeth rose to help, and turned in surprise when she heard a footstep outside in the hall. Then she stood rooted to the spot, staring unbelievingly at the vision confronting her. The others followed her gaze. Standing upon the threshold of the room was Julia. Her face wore a wide, wide grin, and spikes and tufts of hair framed it like the wig of a rag doll. Beside her was Nicholas, also grinning. A battery of kirbigrips sticking out round his ears like the prickles of a porcupine secured two long brown plaits to his scalp.

V

The night before, Julia had gone to bed with a pair of curved nail scissors under her pillow. Had not mummy said, in front of that trusty witness Aunt Beth, " You can have your hair off tomorrow as far as I'm concerned?" Well, she would wait until tomorrow was today, and then off it would come, before her mother changed her mind.

One plait was already off when Inspector Howard came into the children's bedroom early in the morning, hence her cocoon-like position in the bed; later she had enlisted Nick's aid to achieve a professional trim round the back. Julia had looked at her reflection in high delight in the mirror before coming downstairs to dazzle her family.

Susan had thought Julia's shrinking under the bedclothes earlier had been due to alarm, and was now on the point of going to reassure her daughter. She looked at her, thunderstruck at finding the true explanation so plainly different.

" Julia, you naughty, wicked little girl," she began to scold, her cheerful control snapping. She caught hold of the child angrily; this was the final straw.

"Oh, don't be cross with her, Susan," begged Mrs. Trent, wiping her eyes with a handkerchief. "That's exactly what we need now, a good laugh." She sat back in her chair unable to stop laughing.

Julia, round-eyed, looked from one to the other of the grown-ups. It was clear that her surprise had not had the desired effect. Hugh hid a smile behind his hand; there was no doubt that the child looked a sight, but in time the hair would grow and she'd certainly shown initiative in gaining her object.

Susan released her and stood looking at her helplessly. No amount of anger would put the plaits back again. Muttering crossly she began to unpin them from the protesting Nicholas.

Elizabeth saw the crestfallen expression on Julia's face and came to the rescue.

"It looks very nice, dear," she said, stifling the near hysterical mirth she felt now at the comic spectacle of the two children. "Why, it's just like mine."

VI

Half an hour later the two sisters-in-law were in the kitchen, breakfast ready, and dressed to face the day. By now Susan had recovered her good humour and was able to see the funny side of Julia's drastic deed.

"Well, she's certainly given us something else to talk about," she said, chuckling. "But what a sight she looks! It'll take ages to grow to a respectable length."

"She's cut it all lopsided," agreed Elizabeth. "I expect Nick helped. Oh, I'd have loved a snapshot of them standing there; Nick looked wonderful with the plaits on. And just when we were all feeling so tense! If you like, Sue, I'll have a go at tapering off a few of those chunky ends, it might improve it a bit."

"By all means, do anything you like," said Susan. "It could hardly be worse; I should imagine anything would improve it. She'll have to wear a hat at the Flower Show."

" It won't seem so queer when we get used to it," suggested Elizabeth optimistically.

Just then Hugh, spruce and brushed, came into the kitchen. Well trained, he offered to help and was set to making the toast.

" You're very smart, Hugh," said Susan in surprise, seeing that he was wearing his tidy suit.

Hugh exchanged a glance with Elizabeth and coughed, in some embarrassment.

" I, er, I just thought it would save changing later," he said carelessly.

Susan frowned. She had seen the look.

" There's some mystery here, Hugh Bellamy," she declared, " and you haven't told me yet how you knew about Victor. Come on, out with it."

" I think we'd better tell her, Elizabeth," said Hugh sheepishly. " After all, she must have had a rough time yesterday when the police were here. He didn't tell us she'd been with them."

" He didn't tell you? Who didn't tell you?" pounced Susan sharply. " Do you mean you saw Victor too?"

She spoke loudly, and they all started guiltily and looked round as if Inspector Howard might be lurking under the table.

" Too? Then you saw him, Susan?" asked Elizabeth incredulously.

Susan shook her head. " Luckily for him I didn't, but I knew last night that he was in the cellar," she said. " Also luckily for him I didn't know he was there yesterday morning when the police came. Mummy found him when she went down there after tea to fetch a flower bowl."

" Good gracious! Then that was why she was so pale at dinner! No wonder!" exclaimed Elizabeth. " Oh, how dreadful!"

Susan nodded. " That's why I suggested canasta, so that she could take him down some food and have a chat without the rest of you knowing," she said complacently. " You nearly caught us, Elizabeth, do you remember, when you came into the kitchen? We said we were planning the food for today but really we'd been making sandwiches for him."

"Why, the low-down little rat," said Hugh, looking very angry. "Sorry, Elizabeth, but he did behave pretty badly."

Susan looked puzzled. "But I don't understand what you're talking about," she said.

Elizabeth explained. "I knew he was in the cellar all the time," she said. "He came here on Saturday night. I took him some food, and last night he came into the house to have a bath because he got so dirty hiding under the coke. Hugh heard us in the kitchen. But Victor never said he'd seen you or mother. In fact Hugh really only let him go so that no one else would be involved."

"And you gave him your flannels and jacket, I suppose?" said Susan to her husband.

Hugh nodded.

"And money?" she went on. "And I suppose that's why you wanted money too, Elizabeth?"

"Yes," agreed Elizabeth.

Everything had fallen into place now. They thought it over for a moment, seeing their deceptions in a new light. Then Susan began to laugh.

"Well, we're all accessories now," she said. "Poor Daddy was the only one surprised to see the police. I think we were mad not to give Victor up, but even so, thank you, Hugh. I didn't know you had it in you, and how horrid you were to that nice inspector." She stood on her toes and gave her startled husband a resounding kiss. "Well, I only hope he's miles away from here by now."

VII

Breakfast at the Priory was eaten to the accompaniment of much forced hilarity. Susan surpassed herself cracking jokes and imagining all the unlikely things that might happen to make the day memorable, as if it were not that already. Elizabeth and Hugh did their best to support her, and every time there was a lull in the conversation one of them rushed into the breach with a remark, not caring if it was foolish so long as it filled the gap.

The brigadier alone was silent, wading through his bacon and egg very slowly, as though every mouthful tasted of sawdust.

Julia sat in unusual meekness, with her tufted hair unevenly haloing her small head. With a child's perception she sensed the extraordinary atmosphere round the table; vaguely she supposed it had some connection with her shorn locks. She had forgotten all about the policemen's visit.

Suddenly her grandfather noticed that there was something different about the little girl.

"Why, Julia, you've cut your hair!" he remarked in surprise.

"Yes, grandfather," she answered in a subdued voice, aware by now that her act had not met with wholehearted adult approval.

"Speak up, child, speak up," ordered the brigadier. "Never could stand mumbling. Well, hold your head up and let's have a look at it."

Obediently Julia raised her downcast eyes and staunchly met his critical regard.

"Hm, well, you haven't made a very professional job of it, I can see that," he said when he had subjected her to a steady scrutiny. Then a smile quirked the corner of his mouth. "But never mind, I like it. It's an improvement. Susan, I'm glad to see your daughter has some determination and spirit."

Everyone looked a little startled at the vigorous way he spoke, and a wave of relief spread round at his return to normal.

"Now, we must make plans for the day," he went on briskly. "What time are all these people coming to luncheon?"

"At a quarter to one, dear, in time for sherry," said Mrs. Trent. "We must eat punctually at one or we'll be late at the Show and that would never do. We must get Harley Darrell down there in good time."

"Well, you leave the food to Elizabeth and me," said Susan, "and you go down to the marquee and arrange your flowers."

"Will you be able to manage?" asked Mrs. Trent. "I couldn't ask Mrs. Meaker to come up today when she's only just started to work here."

"No, of course not. We'll manage easily," said Susan with more confidence than truth.

"Granny?" said Julia hesitantly.

"What, my pet?" asked Mrs. Trent.

"Can I go in for the flowers-in-a-saucer competition?"

"Yes, certainly you can, dear," said her grandmother.

"And me," said Nicholas, not to be outdone. Though now to his regret plaitless, he had instead a fine eggy beard and moustache adorning his round face.

"And you, too, Nick," agreed Mrs. Trent. "You can be busy picking them while Mummy and Aunt Elizabeth are getting lunch ready."

As she finished speaking, she rose to go and see about her flowers, and Hugh said he would bring the car round for her to take everything down to the village.

"Do you think it's all right for her to go alone, in case people say anything to her?" Susan whispered to Elizabeth.

"Oh, yes, she'll manage," said Elizabeth. "I'm sure she'd rather we didn't fuss. Look how brave she was last night, she'll carry it off."

They went in to the kitchen to begin the long task of washing up and preparing for the buffet luncheon. The newspapers had already been poked through the back door by Billy Brown, and Susan brought them in. She glanced quickly through them, and when she saw the reference to Victor she hid them in a drawer of the dresser.

"It'll be just as well if Daddy doesn't see these," she said to Elizabeth. Then she looked at her sister-in-law curiously. "Are you very upset yourself?" she enquired.

Elizabeth gave her a rueful smile. "I don't really know," she confessed. "Rather frightened, in case we have a lot of trouble, and very angry. But not sad."

Susan gave her a shrewd glance. "If he does get away, it lets you out, doesn't it?" she asked.

Elizabeth nodded, without speaking.

"Then I hope to goodness he succeeds," said Susan fervently. "That's the one ray of light in this otherwise black business. You know my views on that subject."

Elizabeth smiled. "I do, Sue, and I don't mind admitting what a reprieve it will be."

"We'll hold our thumbs," said Susan. "There is a chance, I suppose. He's got plenty of money, you say, and he seems to have organised the whole thing pretty thoroughly."

"If only his nerve holds," said Elizabeth.

"Yes," agreed Susan. "You must have had an awful fright in the night when Hugh found you."

"I did," said Elizabeth with a shudder. "But he was splendid, Sue, once he agreed to help. He even gave me some brandy because I was a bit strung up."

Susan laughed. "He didn't tell me that bit," she said. "But he always believes in a nip in times of crisis."

"Well, it just about saved me," Elizabeth admitted.

"Poor Hugh, it's awful for him, all this," said Susan more seriously. "He must have hated being so unhelpful to the inspector this morning. He's never had any sympathy for Victor as you know, and he's the last person to try and thwart the course of justice."

"I know," said Elizabeth. "Whether Victor gets away or not, I'll always be grateful to Hugh for what he's done, because it was such an awful lot to ask of him."

They were silent then, still busy washing up, and while they were thus employed Mrs. Meaker came into the kitchen.

"I thought Mrs. Trent would be needing some help today, with all those people to lunch and one thing and the other," she announced, taking an apron out of her holdall and tying it firmly round her waist. One glance at the morning's paper had been enough to make her come at once to offer the only help within her power.

"How good of you, Mrs. Meaker," said Susan gratefully, realising from the way she spoke that she had seen the news. "My mother will be glad, there is a lot to do."

"That's what I thought, miss," said Mrs. Meaker, who had known Susan since she was in her pram. "Now you let me finish those plates, I'm sure you've plenty to do." She plunged her strong bare arms into the sink of hot, soapy water and Susan moved away to consult with Elizabeth over salads.

They were interrupted by the telephone. It was Lady Faversham, who sounded embarrassed when she found it was Elizabeth who had answered.

"I really wanted to speak to Mrs. Trent," she explained rather awkwardly.

"I'm afraid she's out just now. She's gone to arrange her flowers in the marquee," said Elizabeth. She sounded so calm that Lady Faversham was further disconcerted.

"Well, I wondered if I could help in any way," she said at last. "Perhaps you would like me to have the luncheon here?"

Elizabeth understood and felt a surge of gratitude. How kind people were! First Mrs. Meaker and now this; she knew it would not be easy for Lady Faversham to undertake the lunch party at such short notice.

"It's very kind of you, Lady Faversham," she said sincerely. "My mother-in-law will be so grateful when I tell her, but we're going to carry on just as usual; it isn't going to make any difference."

"You're certain, Elizabeth? You're sure it's all right?" Lady Faversham was relieved but astonished.

"Yes, really, thank you so much," said Elizabeth. "There is one thing, though; I wonder if you would be very kind and lend us some sherry glasses and some tumblers? We had a disaster last night and broke a trayful."

"Of course I will. I'll bring them with me. Will a dozen of each do?" asked Lady Faversham.

"That would be lovely, thank you so much," said Elizabeth.

"You're sure there's nothing else?"

"Quite sure," said Elizabeth. "But thank you again for suggesting it."

"Well, tell your mother-in-law to ring me if there's anything at all we can do, won't you?" said Lady Faversham, still feeling that there must be something.

"I will," said Elizabeth. After this conversation she sud-

denly felt exhausted, and remembered her discussion with
Susan. She supposed she must be more upset than she had
thought. Hugh came into the drawing-room as she replaced
the telephone, and she turned to speak to him.

"Hugh, where do you think he is now?" she asked.

He shrugged.

"Goodness knows," he said. "With luck a hundred miles
away, if he got on early train. Anyway he's got enough food
for several days; he'll be able to keep clear of cafés, and it's
warm enough to sleep out. I should think there's a good chance
he will get away. He's got money, you see. It's lack of food
and money that gives these chaps away. I must say I hope he
does succeed or we shall be in for trouble when they do catch
him."

"But he wouldn't say we'd helped," protested Elizabeth,
without much conviction.

"I shouldn't rely on that," said Hugh grimly. "But still,
it won't help to brood about it, Elizabeth. Best try not to think
of it. Anyway, I hope for your sake he gets away, you're well
rid of him."

She looked sad for a moment. Then she smiled.

"We must try to forget it—you're right, Hugh," she said.
"We must cheer up. After all, it's a holiday and we mustn't
get swamped in gloom. Now I must go back and help
Susan."

Fifteen minutes later the telephone rang again. This time it
was Richard.

"Oh, Beth, I've been so anxious about you," he began at
once when he heard Elizabeth's voice.

"It's all right, Richard, there's nothing to worry about,"
she said quickly. "The police have been here, searching, but
of course there was nothing to find."

"No, of course not," he agreed doubtfully. Could the Trents
really not know that Victor had been in Bramsbourne? "But
what a shock for you all," he said. "Are you all right? Shall
I come round?"

"No, really Richard, it's all right," said Elizabeth. "They've
all been wonderful and everything is to go on just as though

nothing had happened. Mother's gone down to the marquee with her flowers."

"Has she? How splendid," said Richard. "I'll see her there, then. If you do want me, Beth, I'll be there all the morning, I've fetched the buns for tea already. You will send for me if there's anything I can do, won't you?"

"I will, Richard. Thank you very much for ringing. We'll meet at lunch."

"Yes. Don't worry too much, Beth. I'm sure he's miles away from here by now," said Richard.

"I won't," said Elizabeth. "Goodbye till lunch time."

"Till then," said Richard. "Goodbye, Beth."

They hung up, and Elizabeth went slowly back to the kitchen, suddenly thoughtful. Richard had said, "He's miles away from here by now." She remembered his visit at tea time yesterday and the anxious glances he had given her. It was as though he had known all the time that Victor had been near.

VIII

When the first faint streaks of dawn lightened the sky, Victor had slipped down the garden and across the brook. He carried the small case containing his provisions, and his pocket bulged with banknotes. Over the fields he moved, swiftly and surely, keeping to the shelter of the hedges, remembering every inch of the way clearly from his boyhood. He was frightened now, out on his own again, but still confident of success.

A few cocks crowed and soon the waking birds began to twitter, but otherwise all was quiet and no human stirred. The air smelled fresh and clean and sweet at this early hour.

At last he came to where he must cross the first road; he crouched down behind the hedge, making sure that all was clear, and as he did so a police car went quietly past. Victor's heart pounded; he squatted down, holding his breath, but it drove slowly on. He had not been seen. On he went, over the

fields the other side of the road; it was getting warmer now
and he began to sweat. Presently he stopped near a haystack
and opened his case; it was time for some breakfast. It was
while he was sitting there, eating sandwiches, that he realised
he had not collected the money Richard was to have left in
the churchyard.

"Oh, never mind," he thought in annoyance, "I'll have
to go on without it."

But as he resumed his walk, he could not put the thought
of that twenty pounds out of his mind. Supposing his whole
escape failed simply for want of such a sum! How foolish to
be beaten because of twenty pounds that were waiting to be
collected.

Victor turned about and began walking back towards
Bramsbourne.

IX

Hugh helped his mother-in-law to load her vases and flowers
into the boot of the car. She took a bucket half full of water
and a small watering can as well.

"Won't it spill?" asked Hugh, dubiously eyeing this queer
cargo which he had placed at her instruction on the floor in
the back.

"Oh, no, not if I go slowly," she reassured him cheerfully.
"It's such a long way to the nearest tap down there, so I
always take some water every year."

"Well, if you're sure," said Hugh, still doubtfully. "You
wouldn't like me to come with you? I could fetch the water
for you," he offered helpfully.

"No, thank you, Hugh, I'll be all right," she said. She got
into the driving seat and switched on the ignition. The engine
started easily, and with a leap as she let the clutch abruptly
in, Mrs. Trent was gone. Hugh watched her go with admiration. It took courage to face alone the whispers and sympathetic glances she could expect today.

All was bustle at the Big Meadow when Mrs. Trent arrived.
She steeled herself, for Victor's escape would certainly be in

today's papers; there would be no kind enquiries, but instead strained efforts at normality and avoidance of question. But perhaps Billy Brown was not delivering any papers today, she thought hopefully. There seemed to be none at the Priory, and as he was notoriously a lazy boy there was a possibility that he would take the day off.

She got out of the car. Alas, Hugh was right, and water had slopped from the bucket on to the worn carpet in the back. She sighed. This happened every year, but every year she still hoped to arrive smoothly and without spilling a drop. She lifted the bucket out and began to carry it across the field towards the big marquee. A hum of many voices like the buzzing of a beehive came across the air from all the busy people inside it. When Mrs. Trent entered the gloom of the tent there was sudden silence : then the talk broke out again with even greater zest.

So they do know, she thought heavily, blinking in the dimness. They had all been discussing it till she walked in. She lifted her head, remembering what she had said earlier, that there was no new disgrace so that this need not be an ordeal like the trial. She put down her bucket and said good morning brightly; then she admired a spray of clarkia which Miss Finch was holding comtemplatively aloft like the angel Gabriel with his lily. She returned to the car for her basket of flowers, and began to arrange them in the vases she had brought as she had planned to do last night, before she knew of Victor's presence. Only Mrs. Maggs, busy spreading out the needlework exhibits on another table saw how her hands trembled.

Soon the marquee began to fill with colour. There were long trestles all round the sides, standing end to end and laden with flowers, fruit and vegetables. On centre tables the bottled fruit and jam were marshalled, with the cakes and handwork, all neatly labelled. When their arranging was finished and everything was displayed to the best advantage the proud owners hovered about, reluctant to abandon their precious entries and excitedly anticipating the moment when the judges would ponderously decide their rival merits. Now there was still time to dream of victory; this afternoon all would be

irrevocably determined and the defeated must sportingly con-
gratulate the modest winners whilst abandoning all thought
of glory for another year.

In a smaller tent outside, the good ladies in charge of the
catering arrangements were busy setting out crockery and
glasses which Richard had hired and fetched from Haverstoke. Today, as soon as he had finished breakfast, he had
driven in again to collect trays of buns and cakes that had
been brought with Flower Show funds and now he was jour-
neying back and forth from the tent to his car carrying them
to his willing helpers. Bert Higgs was supplying from the Rose
and Crown quantities of fizzy fruit squashes on a sale-or-return
basis, and an ice cream van was expected during the afternoon. Everything was well organised and under way; even
Ivy Higgs was there, helping to wash cups and making sure
the ancient oil stoves would boil the water successfully. A few
excited children hovered about getting in the way of their
elders, or ran to gaze at the brightly coloured roundabout
which was ready in the bottom corner of the field. Dad had
run the motor and tested the loudspeaker; now he was going
round with a huge oil can giving the mechanism a few last
drops for luck.

At last Mrs. Trent's share of the work was done, and she
could return home with just time to change in comfort before
she must meet the judges at the scene of their deliberations.
She picked up her bucket and gardening basket, and was
walking back over the grass to the road when Richard came
up to her.

"Let me take those, Mrs. Trent," he said, relieving her
of her load. "Your flowers look lovely, you should easily win
the sweet pea class."

She smiled. "I doubt it," she said. "Violet Faversham's are
always better. I see she isn't bringing them till the last
moment."

"Perhaps it will be your turn to win this year," suggested
Richard. "I hope you do." He opened the door of the car to
put the basket and bucket inside.

"Look at that water. Hugh will be cross, he told me it

would spill," said Mrs. Trent. " I always bring a bucket of water, it's such a long way to the tap."

" I'll mop it up a bit," said Richard. He found a cloth in the pocket of the car. " Can I use this?"

She nodded, and he began to wipe up the flood, absorbing some into the oily rag and sweeping most of it out over the running board. A good deal had been blotted up by the strip of mat. Then he put her things back, and opened the door for her. Mrs. Trent got in once more.

" Let me know if there's anything I can do, won't you?" said Richard, shutting her in. She smiled at him gratefully, knowing he was not simply referring to the day's activities. How like Richard not to bother one with a lot of platitudes, but simply to make instead a sincere and practical statement.

" I will, Richard," she promised, and drove away, this time smoothly and without a jerk. " Just because the bucket is empty and no critical Hugh is watching," she thought ruefully.

X

During a brief lull in the morning, while Mrs. Meaker washed lettuces, boiled eggs and skinned tomatoes, and Susan stood over the refrigerator willing the jellies and mousse inside it to set, Elizabeth summoned Julia into the garden and sat her upon a stool under the shade of the copper beech tree. She wrapped a towel cloakwise round the child's neck and handed her a mirror in which to watch proceedings. Then, with a comb in one hand and her father-in-law's special moustache-trimming scissors in the other, she set about improving Julia's hair.

" I thought it looked like the smooth cut in your magazine," offered the child helpfully; she sat very still.

" It looks more like the ragged doll cut," said Elizabeth bluntly. " There's not much we can do about it till it grows a bit. You were a chump to do it yourself. No one can see the back of their own head well enough to cut it."

" Me has done the back," declared Nicholas who was an interested spectator of operations.

"So I see," said his aunt grimly, busily tapering a particularly bushy lump by Julia's right ear.

"Well, it's off anyway," said the shorn one cheerfully. "It'll never grow long now. P'raps Mummy will let me have a perm. A girl at school has," she said hopefully. "Mine is straight, isn't it?" she added with gloom.

"I'm sure Mummy won't let you have a perm till you're at least fifteen," said Elizabeth with conviction. "It's very silly to waste money curling children's hair. As long as it's nicely cut and well brushed it can be very pretty, even if it's straight. I think it just looks ridiculous curled. It's different if it's naturally curly like Nick's."

Julia pouted. "Betty's hair is the nicest in the school," she insisted.

"Nonsense," said Elizabeth, wondering why she was bothering to make such a stand with Julia. "You don't want to wear nylon stockings and high-heeled shoes till you're older, do you?"

"No, of course not, they'd look silly," said Julia.

"Well, so would a perm," Elizabeth told her. She had a horror of little girls guyed up like miniature adults; there lay the way, she felt, to producing problems like Ivy Higgs. She gave a final snip to Julia. "There. Now we'll run upstairs and give it a quick wash, then it won't look so funny," she said.

"But it was only washed on Wednesday, to be clean for the weekend," protested Julia.

"Never mind. It'll shape better if it's washed," said Elizabeth. "The sun will soon dry it. Come along, we must hurry because I ought to be helping Mummy."

"Can we do our flowers when it's washed?" asked Julia.

"Yes, you can," said Elizabeth. "Now hurry."

They went upstairs and she bent Julia over the bathroom basin where she swiftly rinsed the skimpy locks that were left, deaf to agonised cries of water in eyes and ears. She put a grip in the wet hair after it had been rubbed hard in a towel, to hold it out of Julia's face, and gave it a pinch here and there between her fingers.

"Now out you go," she said. "Shoo, and you too, Nick."

After the children had run off she went back to the kitchen. Helping Susan to lay out plates and cutlery, she said, " When you can have Julia's hair properly cut, Sue, I think you'll find it's quite wavy. You have a look when she comes in; there's a strong kink in it."

Susan looked gratified, but made no comment. It was not long before her daughter appeared in the doorway, clutching a bedraggled posy tightly in her small, hot hand, and asking for a saucer in which to arrange it.

" And can I take it down to the tent, or it will miss the judging?" she demanded to know.

" You'd better arrange it down there, Julia," said Susan. She looked critically at her hair. Certainly Elizabeth had improved it, and it was true, there was a strong wave across the shining crown. " You can take them down now; you know the way, don't you? Past the church and down the hill."

" Can I go by myself?" breathed Julia ecstatically. Independence was her cherished goal, but at home where there was more traffic she was rarely allowed out alone.

" Yes, but mind you keep in to the side of the road, out of the way of cars, and don't speak to strangers," warned Susan.

" Nor get into anyone's car nor go for walks with anyone I don't know," intoned Julia solemnly.

" Well, don't," said her mother. " Off you go. Nick, you must stay with us." She gave him a piece of the banana she was slicing for the fruit salad to console him. " There. It really looks as if we might be ready in time after all," she said, and picked up the bowl to carry it into the dining-room.

XI

Julia skipped off down the drive. At the gate she paused for a brief exchange with the policeman on duty, who had lost all interest in his monotonous task, and then she went importantly upon her way. She carried a small basket containing the flowers and two saucers, one of which she would kindly arrange for Nick. Her head felt deliciously light and cool without the weight of her plaits. She waved it about from side to side as she stumped along, like a pony tossing its mane. Presently she got bored with the roadway so she mounted the grass verge, and carried on the pretence of being a pony by jumping over the tiny drain ditches that were cut into it at intervals. Her grandmother came along in the car on her way home from the Big Meadow, and stopped to ask where she was going and to admire the flowers now wilting in the basket. Julia continued on her way, thinking of her return to school and the astonishment of the other girls when they saw her hair. She pondered over Elizabeth's remarks about a perm, and reluctantly decided that as her aunt knew so much about everything that she could write a magazine she must also be right about this.

At last she arrived at the Big Meadow, where there seemed to be dozens of people busily working. As far as she could tell, they were all "strangers" so she could speak to no one, which was a pity since she enjoyed talking. But soon she recognised Mr. Dell and Mrs. Maggs, both of whom seemed pleased to see her, and showed her where to get some water for her saucers, Mrs. Maggs even lending her a jam jar to fetch it in.

Mrs. Maggs watched her solemnly arranging cornflower heads in a circle round a marigold, face rapt in concentration, the tip of her tongue showing at the corner of her mouth.

"Who's been cutting your hair, Julia?" asked the old woman, knowing very well that the little girl had had plaits yesterday.

Julia had the grace to blush. "Well, I did," she confessed, "but Aunt Beth made it better."

"My, whatever next!" exclaimed Mrs. Maggs. "And you so big. Fancy doing such a naughty thing!" She clicked her tongue in the shocked way that had been familiar to generations of children. "Well, never mind; I expect Mummy has scolded you already," she said, relenting. "Here's a sweetie." She offered Julia a fruit drop from a bag out of her pocket. (Only boiled sweets were in her belief harmless to the teeth, and all the children in the village knew that she could be relied on to have some somewhere about her person.)

Julia accepted it, and began frowningly to outline the corn-flowers with snapdragon faces. At last it was finished, with wisps of catmint round the edge, and she embarked upon Nick's contribution. He had provided a large head of cow parsley, one dandelion, three mangled daisies and two pink carnations. With a sigh at this curious assortment of material Julia conscientiously set to work. Richard came to see what she was doing, and she hastily pointed out to him her own more professional display. He too commented on her hair, and was told the story, but with admirable restraint forbore to reprove her. To reward him, Julia announced in the high penetrating voice of an excited child, "And do you know, we've got two policemen at Granny's house! They are nice, one helped me to pick these cornflowers. They've lost something, wasn't it silly of them? They've been looking for them all over Granny's house. Stolen jewels, I expect! I shouldn't think they're there, would you?"

"I'm sure they're not," agreed Richard briskly. At Julia's artless words everyone had paused, hands suspended in the air, halting in their labours, listening in shocked fascination.

Richard took swift action before Julia could say any more.

"Come and see the roundabout," he suggested. "It's all ready to give you lots of lovely rides this afternoon." He took her hand and led her firmly away. As they walked down the hill Dad, warming up as zero hour drew nearer, put on a record, and the strains of *I've got a luvverly bunch of coco-nuts* came stridently out of the loudspeaker, drowning the roar of some aeroplanes that were passing overhead. The air was full of the usual aroma that followed Mum and Dad round Britain, that of spicy frying mixed with the oily fumes of their motor. Julia looked enviously at the dirty children she could see peeping from the bus, where Mum had instructed them all to remain till they had eaten, in case anyone lost his share of the repast through being absent. It must be fun to belong to a fair, she thought.

Richard felt in his pocket, and took out some money. "Here you are, Julia, here's a sixpence each for you and Nick, to

have a ride this afternoon," he said. "Now you'd better run
on home or Mummy will wonder where you are."

"Oh, thank you," cried Julia. She clutched the money in
one grubby hand and her basket in the other, and ran off.
Smiling, Richard watched her small figure in its blue cotton
dress disappearing through the gate; then he walked quickly
back to the tent, where he still had some tasks waiting for
him.

Julia did not hurry up the hill. She was hot, for the tent
had been stuffy. She thought longingly of an ice cream cornet.
If a man came by now with a van, she would buy one, with
her sixpence, in the hope that Granny would finance other
roundabout rides. But no ice cream van came. She decided to
take a short cut through the churchyard, and went in through
the lower gate. It was rather fun skipping about dodging the
graves. Funny to think there were dead people under there.
You musn't walk on them, that would be unkind. But how
could they be under there yet also up with God-in-Heaven?
She sighed, for it was a knotty problem. Never mind, she
wouldn't worry about it now; here was the kerbstone to jump.
Julia hopped over it and in her exuberance dropped her six-
pences. She saw one roll along the gravel path and fall to
rest, but the other one vanished. It was a major calamity. She
searched everywhere; up and down the path she hunted,
losing all common sense and moving far away from where
the mishap had occurred. Nearing the water butt, her fingers
found a loose stone. She moved it in case the sixpence was
behind it : there, confronting her, was a large white envelope.
Nothing was written on it, and it was not stuck up. Julia knew
you must never open other people's letters, but this wasn't
a letter, and anyway it wasn't fastened. Slowly she opened it.
Inside there were lots and lots of pounds! Her eyes opened
wide : buried treasure! She forgot all about the missing sixpence and put the envelope into her basket. Then she got to
her feet and hurried off towards the gate. She was tiny, and
the man coming from the opposite direction did not see her
behind the wall. They collided and he almost knocked her over
as he pushed roughly past. For a moment he looked at her in

shocked surprise; then he ran down the path and disappeared round the side of the church. Julia stared after him in bewilderment; then she remembered her exciting discovery and hastened back to the Priory.

XII

Susan and Elizabeth had gone upstairs to change when Julia arrived. She went straight to her mother, holding out the envelope.

"Look, Mummy, look what I found! Buried treasure!" she cried.

Puzzled, Susan took it and looked inside.

"Julia! Where did you get this?" she exclaimed. She took the notes out and counted them. Twenty pounds!

Julia told her tale rather incoherently, but by patient cross-examination Susan eventually understood how she had discovered the package.

"Won't we be able to have lots of rides on the roundabout now," chortled the little girl gleefully.

Susan did not answer. She went to the door and called, "Elizabeth, can you come here a minute?"

Elizabeth came at once, doing up the belt of her linen dress as she hurried down the passage.

"Come in and shut the door," directed Susan, looking serious.

In some surprise, Elizabeth complied.

Susan showed her the money. "Now tell Aunt Beth where you found it," she instructed Julia. Obediently the child repeated her story, glancing uncomprehendingly from one grave grown-up face to the other. "Oh, and as I was coming out of the gate a rough man pushed past me," she remembered. "I expect he was one of those bad man you told me about, Mummy," she added cheerfully. "But it didn't matter because he was running away. He had a coat on just like Daddy's."

"Julia, you're not to tell anyone about this, not anyone, not even Daddy," said Susan sternly. "Do you understand?"

Julia stared. "But our rides! It's my money, I found it," she said, and tears began to form.

Susan took a deep breath. "It isn't yours, dear," she said gently. "Someone must have lost it, and you found it. Now they will be wondering where it is. I shall give it to the police if I can't find out whose it is, but tomorrow when we're not so busy."

"There's a policeman outside," Julia pointed out reasonably.

"Well, I think I know who it belongs to," interposed Elizabeth; she looked very serious. "So we won't give it to the police till I've asked the person."

"P'raps somebody dropped it after church," suggested Julia. "But what a pity when it was such good buried treasure."

"Never mind, darling. Daddy will give you some money for lots of rides this afternoon," said Susan. "Now, you won't tell anyone, will you, Julia, about the money or about the man you saw. I don't think he was a horrid man at all, just someone on holiday."

"All right," Julia agreed with reluctance.

"Now go and wash, you're black," said her mother.

The little girl ran out of the room, and the two sisters-in-law regarded one another in silence. Then Elizabeth said, "It must have been Richard who put that money there. He lent me some for Victor and it was in an envelope exactly the same as this."

"But I don't understand," said Susan, looking bewildered.

"Victor must have been to see him and demanded money," said Elizabeth slowly.

"But wouldn't Richard report him?" asked Susan. She saw a faint rush of colour rise into Elizabeth's pale cheeks and as suddenly subside, and remembered her mother's disclosure yesterday.

"He might have wanted to spare us more distress," said Elizabeth.

"I see," answered Susan. "Well, thank goodness he can have his money back anyway."

"It must have been Victor whom Julia saw," went on Elizabeth. "I thought he'd be miles away by this time."

"Is it likely he'd clear out and leave twenty smackers behind?" asked Susan practically. "You know Victor wouldn't miss the chance of five bob."

"What can he have been doing all the morning?" wondered Elizabeth.

"Dodging the cops, I should think," said Susan vulgarly. "Anyhow, we can't possibly do anything, Elizabeth. Best try not to think about it. We'll hear soon enough if they catch him in Bramsbourne."

"Let's hope Julia keeps quiet," said Elizabeth. "It's terrible to involve a child in a thing like this."

"She doesn't understand. Don't worry," said Susan soothingly. "I almost wish they'd catch him and then we could all relax. The suspense is awful."

"I wish I'd given him up when he first came," said Elizabeth slowly. "It's all got too big, there are too many people involved. If he's still so near it must only be a matter of time." All her hopes were fast disappearing. Soon Victor would be back behind bars, and nothing would be changed, except that there might be an added amount of trouble for those who had helped him. But talking would not help; they must still get ready for the luncheon party even if it never took place.

XIII

The superintendent scratched his head and looked perplexedly at Inspector Howard.

"And you mean to tell me that he slipped through your fingers when he was right under your nose?" he demanded with fine contempt for metaphor. "What are you thinking of, Howard? Are you sure he really was in the cellar?"

"Well, that coke had been disturbed," the inspector insisted. "The air in the cellar was full of dust when I went in there with the young woman, Mrs. Bellamy, yesterday morning. That isn't natural in summer, when it isn't being used, now is it, sir?" he asked reasonably. He was so disappointed at having failed thus far in his quest for Victor that he looked like a crestfallen small boy.

"Hum; I suppose not," admitted the superintendent. "Pity you didn't think of it at the time. Go on."

"We had it all turned over this morning," continued the inspector, "but there wasn't a trace of him, not a trace. He must have got clean away in the night."

"But do you think the Trents knew he was there? Were they hiding him? Is that your theory?" asked the superintendent.

"I just don't know," confessed Inspector Howard. "I thought Mrs. Bellamy looked a bit upset yesterday, but so would anyone if they'd just heard their brother was on the loose again. She couldn't have been more helpful about my searching the place. And the others this morning, they all seemed quite astonished. If they did know anything they're all damned good actors."

"It seems so odd that they hadn't heard of his escape," said the superintendent.

"Why should they hear? Only a few of the later papers carried names and descriptions, and with the house full they might not have had time for reading."

"Well, I just can't understand it," sighed the superintendent. "We've lost all trace of him since the fair people dropped him on Saturday afternoon. He can't have vanished, he'd need food and so on. Of course Hopkins at Bramsbourne is about the most brainless copper in the force; if you're right about young Trent being in the cellar, he could have walked right past Hopkins on his way to the Priory without being recognised."

"He's not very bright, certainly," agreed the inspector. "All the same," he added reflectively, "he did report about young Mrs. Trent cashing a cheque at the grocer's yesterday. That seems a funny thing for her to do on a Sunday when she's on holiday. And an efficient, practical young woman I'd judge her to be, not the type to forget to go to the bank before coming away for the weekend. I wonder why she did it? Then, Mrs. Bellamy asked me if we'd caught the other man, so she must have known that two had escaped. No, I'm convinced I'm right about him being in that cellar, and I suspect the people at the Priory are not as ignorant about it all as they'd have us believe."

"Well, find Trent, that's all I ask," said the superintendent grimly. "I don't care where he is as long as he's found. As well as all this business we're sure to have several accidents to cope with since it's a fine Bank Holiday; then we need every available man for all the fêtes and garden parties there are today. Got that film star Harley Darrell coming to Bramsbourne, haven't they? There's sure to be a box up with the traffic there, then. And now you want to take all my men to comb the district for a convict you ought to have bagged last night. I don't know what things are coming to. I don't know why I ever became a policeman, I ought to have been a bank clerk, then I could take the day off like everyone else. Well, Howard, get moving, and for goodness sake find some clue as to where he's gone from here, for gone he has by now."

"I'll do my best, sir," said Inspector Howard sadly. He picked up his cap, and, looking very thoughtful, left the office.

XIV

Ivy decided : "I'll give him one more chance. I'll phone up before I get young Mrs. Trent to introduce me to Harley Darrell." Accordingly she telephoned Alan's aerodrome, but without success. On that bright holiday Monday he was nowhere to be found.

Disappointed, she hung up the receiver. Then she thought more hopefully, perhaps he's on his way over here, to plead with me again, at the Flower Show. With a strange new softening of her heart she planned to lead him on a bit, and then to say, maybe. But all the time she could not put the thought of Harley Darrell out of her head. Dizzy images still spun around in her woolly little brain, dreams of herself mincing along on stilt-high heels among a mink-clad throng, and visions of her sultry photograph on cinema hoardings. She sighed, for she did not really know what she wanted.

It was time to get ready, for whatever the future she must be at the Meadow in good time. She went upstairs to her bedroom, where her yellow sprigged organdie dress hung waiting in the wardrobe. It had a stiff rustling taffeta petticoat that was very alluring. Ivy began to take off her faded cotton working dress, preparing for the fray.

XV

The judging was a solemn business. A procession, led by the gardening expert whose responsibility it was, and consisting of Brigadier and Mrs. Trent, Richard, and various other dignitaries of Bramsbourne's horticultural life, went silently round the big marquee. Everything was scrutinised from all angles; each bean runner was held to the light, fingered and measured; each pea pod weighed in the hand. Every vegetable had reached such monster size that when cooked it would be tough and tasteless, but for the sake of the show size was all that mattered.

With due ceremony notes were made and the coveted tickets of victory laid beside the triumphant exhibits. At last it was finished and everyone went back to the Priory, except Richard who was waylaid by Miss Finch. She was hopping about outside the marquee like an agitated sparrow, unable to bear the suspense of waiting for the results of the " Flower Poetry " class. Richard was able to tell her that her entry was second; and pleased, yet a little deflated for she had hoped to win, she went back to her cottage to get ready for the afternoon.

Richard made his way back to the vicarage to wash and change out of his flannels into a suitable clerical suit, for there had not been time this morning. However quick he was, he was bound to be late for the lunch party, so like Julia earlier he took the short cut through the churchyard.

Coming along the path by the water butt he decided to see whether Victor had been to collect the money; if so there was hope that by now he was well away from Bramsbourne. He bent and felt beneath the loose stone where yesterday he had hidden the envelope. There was nothing there. Richard felt heartily thankful. It was always hard for him to pass his beloved church without slipping inside for a moment, and now in his relief he did so again, knowing that the few minutes thus used in refreshing himself would be more than made up for later in the day. As always when the sunlight was so bright it seemed dark inside, but a sudden sound near the curtain behind which the bier was kept attracted his attention. Frowning, for no mouse had made the noise, Richard walked over and pulled the curtain quickly aside. Behind it, crouching against the wall, Victor glared at his discoverer.

For a moment both men were silent and motionless. Then Victor relaxed and stood up while Richard fell back a pace, still holding the end of the curtain.

"So you're still here," he said at last, the first to speak.

"Why didn't you bring the money?" asked Victor angrily, relief at seeing Richard and not the police giving way to frustrated rage.

"I did bring it. I thought you'd taken it," Richard said.

"I came for it, but it wasn't there," said Victor in a surly voice.

"Then someone else must have found it," said Richard. "Did anyone see you coming? Was there anyone in the churchyard when you got there?"

Victor shook his head. "No, only a kid, a little girl."

Richard remembered Julia. "Did she have very short hair and a blue frock?" he asked.

The other nodded. "I believe she did."

"That was your niece, Julia," said Richard grimly. "I wonder if she could have found it?" He was thinking that whoever had discovered it would think it very odd that an envelope of treasury notes should be hidden in a churchyard.

"I believe she was carrying something," Victor said. "She had a basket with a book or a packet in it, I noticed it when I passed her. She gave me a turn, so I hurried by. What a pity, I could have got it from her easily."

Richard knew that Julia's basket had been empty when she left the Meadow this morning. He shuddered inwardly at the evil look on Victor's face and gave silent thanks that she had escaped whatever terror her uncle in his blind fear might have brought her.

"Well, you've lost it now, at all events," he said shortly. He thought of the police whom he had seen patrolling in fast cars round the lanes. There was small hope now of Victor getting through undiscovered, anyway till nightfall. He took a sudden decision.

"You must stay here today," he said. "I'll come back this evening when the Flower Show is over and take you to Haverstoke in my car. The police won't search it, they all know me. I'll drop you there and then you can get on by yourself. You haven't a hope in daylight."

"Are you on the level?" asked Victor incredulously. "You won't go from here and give me up?"

"No, I won't," said Richard. "You can trust me. You'll be safe here, but stay hidden till I come tonight. Now I must go." He let the curtain fall into place again and hurriedly left the church.

XVI

None of the luncheon party guests, with the exception of Harley Darrell, was surprised to find a large policeman standing at the entrance to the Priory drive. Very politely he stopped each car and peered within, in case Victor should be lurking on the floor.

In the house, Elizabeth and Susan were waiting with smiling faces to greet Lady Faversham and the other visitors, while Hugh was ready with a cocktail shaker filled with a mixture potent enough to relax the embarrassment everyone was feeling.

Harley, as planned by his publicity agent, was the last to arrive. Silent and gleaming, his Bentley drew to a graceful halt in the prepared space on the gravel sweep, and smiling graciously, the film star emerged, speckless from head to foot in his perfectly tailored light grey suit, his grey silk tie to match and his snowy silk shirt. Slim and spruce, he advanced towards his old friend Violet Faversham who stood at the front door with Mrs. Trent waiting to perform introductions. These over, he paused with suave courtesy for the ladies to precede him into the house. He was used to meeting quantities of strangers whose names he seldom caught, and he was also adept at conducting interminable conversations with his admirers without paying the least attention to what was said; but on this occasion his fame meant little to most of his fellow guests, who rarely visited the cinema, and if they did it was seldom to the sort of film in which he played; therefore today he was as welcomed more in the role of the Favershams' friend than that of an idol of the silver screen, a new and pleasant situation.

Hugh's cocktail was good and Harley enjoyed it; it was clean and tangy, not one of the sickly concoctions so often offered. It seemed a good party, he thought, hearing the high buzz of conversation round him and noticing the busy way everyone was talking. He could not know that all were determined never to let a moment's silence occur. He was introduced to the gardening expert who had just completed his judgment in the marquee; he was a little, elderly man with a shiny bald head and pince-nez, bent and gnarled like one of his own ancient apple trees. It was hard to find a point of contact with him until Harley was inspired to comment on his hostess's flowers, which opened the conversational gates, and the famous horticulturist ended by seeking out his equally gnarled and bent little wife to tell her that these film chaps weren't so bad after all when you got to know them.

Harley recognised Elizabeth, easily remembering her since her quiet grace had impressed him at their other meetings. It was a pleasant surprise to find her here, for the name Trent was so general that he had not expected to find any connection between them.

There were too many people to seat for lunch, so the long dining-table had been pulled to one side of the room and there the buffet meal was arranged. In the uninhibited modern manner everyone was loud in praise of the mouth-watering array of food and fell to with gusto. Spearing a piece of

salmon with her fork, Lady Faversham bore down upon
Harley and led him into a corner of the room.

" I must speak to you," she said urgently, " before you make
an unfortunate *gaffe*. That policeman in the road is watching
for the Trents' son who has escaped from prison. I'll tell you
all about it later."

Harley looked startled. " We were stopped several times on
the way here," he said. " Good heavens, how dreadful!"
Then, after a moment's astonished reflection, he asked,
" Would that be the young woman's husband?"

Lady Faversham nodded, without speaking.

" I see; thanks for the warning, Violet," he said with a
grimace. What an extraordinary situation; he wondered what
the story behind it was. Obviously he could not expect to hear
it in this company but must wait for later enlightenment.

Vaguely intending to show sympathy with his host's courage
Harley approached the plainest woman in the room, to whom
he had already been introduced, and who was heartily and
unselfconsciously enjoying a huge plate of cold salmon and
salad in solitary state by the fireplace, and embarked on a
long conversation with her.

Susan and Elizabeth were fully occupied carrying plates
and dishes; in the intervals they kept an eye on Nick and
Julia who sat in splendour at a small table in a corner, tucking
into the delicious food, and in Nick's case liberally casting it
over the cloth and floor.

Richard arrived very late; although she had tried not to
watch for him, Elizabeth knew the instant he came into the
crowded room. By degrees he made his way towards her. He
looked tired; small wonder when the greater part of the or-
ganisation for today devolved upon him. She found Hugh and
asked him to fetch a large gin. Richard accepted it gratefully;
he glanced anxiously at Elizabeth, who seemed entirely calm,
as did the rest of the Trents. Not for the first time Richard
marvelled at the amazing fortitude of humanity.

Elizabeth brought him a well-laden plate.

" I hope you'll like what I chose for you," she said, offering
it to him.

He smiled. " Thank you so much, Beth, it looks lovely. I'm sorry to be so late."

" I expect you've been very busy," she said. She did not bluntly suggest that he should sit down, but gently edged him towards the wall where he could lean unnoticed to rest his leg, and he smiled again, understanding the manœuvre. She saw his face resume its worried look, and said softly, " Richard, I've got an envelope that belongs to you. Julia found it in the churchyard."

He did not know what to say to this, for at all costs Elizabeth must not know how near Victor still was.

" I'm so sorry," she went on simply. " I don't know what he has said to you or what has happened, but it was very good of you, Richard."

" It was nothing," he said. His tone was discouraged and Elizabeth thought he was bothered by his conscience. She glanced round the room; no one was listening to them; everyone was hectically talking. " He'll be miles away by now," she said quietly.

" Of course," said Richard, in the nearest possible approach to a combination of reassurance and truth.

" I must go now, we'll talk later," she said, and with one of her rare smiles she left him.

Richard mechanically ate his lunch, not noticing what it was, and talked meanwhile to whoever came near him; presently he moved to circulate in the throng. All the time his mind was puzzling over the best way to get Victor safely out of the district.

At last the meal was over and the guests began to drift out of the room and into the garden until it should be time to leave for the Show. Julia and Nick, who had been awed by the horde of adults into unusual silence while they ate, now scrambled down from their chairs and went with hopeful spoons amongst the bowls and dishes, " licking," for it seemed a pity to waste so much excellent food. Susan and Elizabeth rescued what they could from these pirate raids and carried it away into the larder, gloomily prophesying imminent biliousness. There was no time to clear up the rest of the debris and the washing up must wait till this evening. They shut the dining-room door upon the sordid scene left by twenty-eight civilised adults and Susan took the children upstairs to be washed. Presently, seraphically spotless, they reappeared, and it was time to leave.

XVI

Lady Faversham was good at speeches. She often had to make them when she presided over committees or opened bazaars; accordingly it was no ordeal for her to mount the platform outside the marquee and introduce Harley Darrell. Very charmingly she did it, looking elegant and distinguished in her pink and black printed silk dress with a large picture hat on her well-blued head.

A polite flutter of applause greeted her words, and as Harley Darrell stepped forward, smiling the famous smile with which he so unfailingly and so frequently seduced Delia Dymple, the clapping swelled into a thunderous roar.

Harley was not very good at speeches, for he was more accustomed to declaiming words of fire or passion that had been composed by someone else. However he looked very romantic and debonair, and that was really all that was required of him. Secretly he felt rather uncomfortable for he had eaten a good lunch with two helpings of trifle and now his stays were making their presence undeniably felt. While he was talking he became aware of a highly coloured young woman in a yellow dress standing in the front row of his audience and regarding him open-mouthed. Though he was used to being stared at, this time it made him feel cross, so he wound up his words swiftly and almost gabbled, " I have much pleasure in declaring this Flower Show open," so that he might move away from her unblinking gaze.

Ivy, for of course it was she, stationed herself for the afternoon a few yards away from her hero, and when he moved, so did she, following him about in best film sleuth fashion, and eager for a chance to catch Elizabeth and get her to carry out the promised introduction.

Everyone began to push frantically into the marquee and along the narrow aisles between the trestles, crowding to see the exhibits and discover who had won prizes. A curious holiday spirit came over Elizabeth and Susan. After their hard work of the morning there was release, and both now were confident that since Victor had not already been found he must be far away, so that their load of anxiety slipped from them. Shedding their years with their cares, they giggled like a pair of schoolgirls over the strange arrangements of some of the competitors.

The winner of the Flower Poetry contest had laid out a complete miniature garden on a tray, titling her entry " A garden is a lovesome thing," and had illustrated the whole poem; there was a rose plot, with small polyantha heads bedded in moss, there was a fern grot, and there was a tiny doll dressed in a morning suit basking in a diminutive deck-chair by a pigmy pool. Susan found this too much for her and had to conceal her merriment in her handkerchief. Miss Finch's second prize was, as might be expected, connected with a gentle passion. Neatly written on a card were the words of Byron :

" My days are in the yellow leaf;
The flowers and fruit of love are gone;
The worms, the canker, and the grief
Are mine alone."

To illustrate this sombre mood a tall branch of yellow box sprouted from one end of a flat bowl, while from the other sprang a deep crimson rose and a spray of late strawberries. In the centre of the arrangement was a sprig from an apple tree, bearing a small diseased fruit upon which crawled a very realistic plasticene worm. Miss Finch, wreathed in joyous smiles, stood proudly near, and it was difficult to compose one's features into a seemly straightness before congratulating her.

Less imaginative but perhaps more decorative, third place was won by Mrs. Trent's " Gather ye rosebuds," a simple bowl of lovely smelling roses.

Julia and Nick soon grew bored following their aunt and

mother round the hot, crowded tent, and even Julia's con-
solation prize for her saucer failed to thrill for long. They
begged urgently for rides on the roundabout. Presently Mrs.
Maggs, having as usual upheld the dignity of the Rectory by
winning the Jam and Bottled Fruits and the Cakes, appeared
and offered to look after the children for a time. Susan
accepted gladly, for though Julia was sensible enough to be
left to herself, Nick still needed constant watching. Happy to
have some young charges again for a brief spell, Mrs. Maggs
went off out of the tent towards the roundabout, whose music
blared invitingly forth *fortissimo*. Dad, dirtier than ever, with
sweat and oil glistening on his face, was at last in his
element.

With her responsibilities temporarily out of her sight, Susan
snooped about the tent, looking at the handicrafts, while Elizabeth followed. Some of the sewing and knitting on display
was exquisite, and they wondered how the busy village women
found time to do such fine work. But it was the vicarage raspberries that had Susan spellbound. The fruit had been
arranged in painstaking symmetry so that only the round inner
hollows showed through the glass.

" What hours it must take to fit them all in like that," she
marvelled. " I should never even think of it, let alone have the
patience."

" Do you suppose she does it like that every time, or just for
the Flower Show?" wondered Elizabeth.

" Let's ask Richard, here he is," said Susan. She turned to
him as he approached. " Richard, we're consumed with curio-
sity to know if Mrs. Maggs always puts the middles of your
raspberries to the outside of the bottles like this," she said.

Richard looked blank. " I couldn't tell you," he replied. He
looked with interest at the victorious bottle. " It is a work of
art," he said admiringly. " I had no idea there was so much
to it, I only know they taste very good in the winter." Although he spoke to Susan his eyes were on Elizabeth; he saw
that the look of strain had gone from her face, and the
laughter she had shared with Susan had brought colour to
her cheeks. She looked young and happy, and he longed for

her to be always so. He thought bitterly of her husband, now skulking in the church, and with dread of what he had planned for tonight. Wrong though it was in some ways, he knew he must do it in a final effort to free Elizabeth from her unhappiness.

"Are you coming to watch the sports?" he asked aloud. "Julia must enter, she'd enjoy it."

"Yes, we'll come. When do they start?" Susan enquired.

"At three-fifteen." Richard glanced at his watch. "It's three o'clock now. I must go down or Bert Higgs will think I'm not coming. I'll see you there."

When he had moved away from them through the press of people, Susan wrinkled up her nose. "Have you ever noticed how unpleasant hot humanity combined with vegetable smells?" she asked in a fastidious voice. "I think Richard's right to move. Let's get out of here, Elizabeth."

XVIII

It was very silent in the church; nothing stirred Occasionally from outside came the twittering of birds, and sometimes a car passed, but mainly all was still. Victor found it eerie, oppressive, unendurable. He ate some of his sandwiches and frightened himself by the small noise of the paper rustling when he unpacked them. Once a very small mouse scampered over the floor making a tiny scuffle, and he started up from his seat with a pounding heart in great alarm.

He wondered what the police were doing, and whether Richard really meant his offer to drive him out of their net, or if it was a trap and he would merely be taken to the nearest police station. Meanwhile the day seemed endless. He wandered round the old building once or twice, but the shadows threatened and the figures of departed saints in the stained windows seemed to stare at him condemningly, so he returned again to his curtained niche.

The events of the past few days were confused in his mind; he remembered the terrifying minutes when he had lain buried under the stifling coke while the police poked about in the cellar; he remembered the long talk he had had with his mother, who had aged greatly in the years since he had seen her. He thought about the small girl he had pushed past this morning; it was odd to reflect that she was his niece, whom he had known as a chubby toddler. If he did get away successfully, these things were memories he would always have, and he would remember his wife. How calm she had remained even on that first night when he had appeared so suddenly at her window. It was Elizabeth's serenity that had first attracted him during the tense days of the war when he had met her; in the midst of a mad world she had seemed sane and he had clung to her poised quietness. It was tragic that he had brought her so low, and genuinely Victor hoped that when he had gone away she would be able to start afresh. Otherwise he felt no repentance for his misdeeds, only for his folly in being found out; his gradual downward progress had obliterated his always meagre sense of right and wrong.

He wondered what the time was. Surely it would be safe to slip outside for a moment to look at the sun and gain some vague idea? He made his way to the door and peered out. All was still. The hot sun beat steadily down on the ancient gravestones, and no breeze stirred the tall beech that stood near the gate. Daringly Victor moved further out; it was good to be in the fresh air, heavy with heat though it was, after the slight mustiness of the church. From away down the hill at the bottom of the village came the distant noise of the Flower Show, with the throb of many voices and the harsh music of the roundabout. Once an aeroplane flew low over the tree tops, shattering the calm with the whine of its engine, and Victor started back into the shadows, then emerged again to watch with a professional eye its swift passage out of sight.

He judged it to be mid-afternoon, getting on for four o'clock. There was still a long time to wait for Richard's return, which perhaps would only mean the end of this brief freedom. He went to the gate and looked about. There was not a soul in sight; if the police were still looking for him here they must be skulking in the bushes. He drew a breath; perhaps they had abandoned the search in this area and moved away. If he decided not to risk waiting for Richard he need waste no more time but could start at once upon his journey. There was no fear of any of Bramsbourne's inhabitants seeing him; they were all down in the Big Meadow and no one was left at home to peep from behind a window curtain and witness him passing. Victor made up his mind. He went back to the church for his case, and a few minutes later he began to walk rapidly down the hill. His way lay through the field next to the Big Meadow, where he could hug the thick hedge for cover, then over the brook and on across the fields to Haverstoke. If he made good time he would be on the train before the Flower Show ended.

XIX

Inspector Howard had cudgelled his brains ever since he left the Superintendent's office, vainly trying to work out where Victor had gone. In spite of his superior's doubt, he was convinced that his theory about the cellar was correct, only where was Victor now? After lunch he returned to the Priory, where his bored constables were still on guard. As he had expected, they had nothing to report. They had looked inside every car that had come to the house, and discreetly questioned every caller. There seemed no remotest connection between this houshold and the escaped convict, except the accident of birth.

The inspector went over it all again in his mind, starting at the beginning when the wanted man had been only ten miles away on Saturday. Surely it was correct to reason that he was on his way home? If he had in fact arrived, then some member of the family must have seen him, but who? All had seemed equally amazed and innocent when questioned this morning. Any discomfiture such as Susan's on Sunday could easily be caused by the shock of the news. But there was Susan's knowledge that two men had escaped; there was the question of Elizabeth's cheque. It would not have been the first time a hunted man's family had banded together to conceal him; and there was no getting away from the evidence of the coke dust; someone had disturbed that coke not long before he had entered the cellar. Slowly the inspector retraced his way there; clump, clump, he descended the stone steps and opened the door. The dust had settled again after his men's work turning over the coke earlier in the day and there was now no trace of it in the atmosphere. There was nothing to be seen, only Mrs. Trent's bulb bowls, and piles of coke. He stood and stared at the boiler, musing. It was antiquated, slightly rusty, silently awaiting its next spell of winter duty. Absent-mindedly, Inspector Howard swung open its heavy iron door. What he saw inside made him utter a muffled exclamation. He put his hand into the boiler and pulled out a very dirty rug, a green thermos flask, and a bundle of soiled greaseproof paper.

XX

This year Mrs. Trent was victorious over Lady Faversham in the sweet pea class, but somehow the longed-for triumph failed to matter. All her thoughts were with her son; she prayed desperately for his escape to succeed; though she knew his punishment was only what he deserved, she could not bear to contemplate it, and now that the chance was here she longed for him to evade such unpleasantness. He must have left the cellar during the night after her talk with him; by now he would be far away.

As Susan had told Elizabeth, she had never visited him in prison for she could not face seeing him in such surroundings, and last night she had found him strangely unchanged. He still possessed the ability to charm, in the way that all his life he had compensated for the defects in his character. She blamed herself now for all that had happened; a firmer resistance to his wiles years back would have forced him to realise that other qualities are necessary. But on the other hand his father had supplied enough sternness and discipline for them both. Where was he now? Where would this all end? Would he manage to get away?

All these things filled her mind as she walked round the

marquee with Harley Darrell, politely talking yet not attending at all to what was said. He was rather enjoying himself, although he had definitely over-eaten and was finding it increasingly warm. He liked the simple, unsophisticated form of the afternoon's programme, which was so different from most of the occasions he graced with his celebrated presence. He was dimly aware of the highly coloured young woman he had noticed during his speech; she still followed him about, but such hangers-on were a familiar part of the scenery. He exerted himself to talk pleasantly to Mrs. Trent, regarding her with amazed respect; it was fantastic that she should be here thus strolling about and conversing so easily while her thoughts must be full of her son.

"Shall we go down and see if the sports have started?" she suggested when they had exhausted the conversational possibilities of dozens of giant vegetable marrows.

Harley agreed, and followed her out of the tent. Ivy, watching, thought it was just like the scene in *Her Blood was Blue,* when he had followed the Lady of the Manor over the sward at a garden party, though on that occasion all were in glorious technicolour costume. She too found time to marvel at Mrs. Trent's composure, for she was not sufficiently modern to shrug and say that such people had no feelings. She fell in behind them as they walked over the dry, springy turf. Elizabeth and Susan came to meet them.

"Julia and Nick are going in for the handicap race," they said. "Come and watch, it's just going to begin." They joined Harley and Mrs. Trent, and all four walked down the hill to the level stretch at the bottom where the runners were being lined up. It was very tricky to arrange the handicaps. Nick, as the youngest entrant, was placed well to the fore with a huge start, bent low ready for the "off," and with a determined look on his face; he seemed to have a clear grasp of what was required of him. Julia, pink with concentration, was somewhere in the middle; her newly shorn hair stood out round her head, glinting in the sun. Richard and Bert Higgs moved briskly amid the ranks of competitors, advancing the position of one and moving another back, determined on fair

play, and privately hoping that no one would collapse with
sunstroke in the intense heat.

Standing by the " rails," Elizabeth suddenly felt her arm
touched, and turned to see Ivy at her elbow.

" Mrs. Trent, you haven't forgotten what you promised,
have you?" she begged, nodding meaningly in the direction
of Harley Darrell, and Elizabeth remembered their conversation yesterday.

" No, of course not, Ivy," she said with her gentle smile.
" Mr. Darrell, may I introduce Miss Ivy Higgs? She is a
great admirer of yours."

Harley turned, wearing his expected smile, and shook Ivy's
trembling hand.

" Oh, please, I want to go to Hollywood, I wrote to you,"
she breathed, losing her assumed poise but not her tongue in
this unique moment.

Harley sighed; he remembered the ill-spelt letter his admirable servant had brought to his notice. To his practised eye,
Ivy looked no less promising than every latest find. He was
sure that under its painted overcoat her skin held the fresh
bloom of youth; her eyes were large and brown; and such of
her hair as was visible beneath her big hat shone with health;
her curving dress clearly contained those attributes so vital to
film allure. There was no reason why she should not be trained
to follow in the long line of glamour girls of whom the public
tired so soon; she could leave her quiet, to him idyllic, village,
and end like him, disorientated, longing for peace, yet using
every artifice to combat approaching age.

" My dear young lady," he said. " You are so pretty that I
feel sure you have a nice young man. Take my advice and
marry him. Settle down in this delightful spot and have a
baby every year. Then you will be happy. In Hollywood you
might find fame, but I doubt if you would find happiness." He
still held her hand, and now he released it with a little bow,
and turned away.

Quick tears sprang to Ivy's eyes. He had snubbed her; have
a baby every year, indeed! What nerve! And he was old, *old*.
His face, seen close to, was lined, and there was grey in his

neatly brushed hair. He even peered at her as though he should be wearing glasses. She turned abruptly, and stumbling on her high heels began hurrying away from the scene of her disillusionment.

Harley watched her go, and turned to Elizabeth with a quizzical expression on his face. " Should I have been more sympathetic?" he asked.

She smiled. " No, I'm glad you did that," she said. " I tried to tell her that it isn't all roses in your profession, but she begged to be introduced. She has got a very nice young man, but her head is so full of the films that she won't think about him. Perhaps she will now; I hope so."

" I'm glad," said Harley. " Of course she'd stand as much chance as anyone else, given an introduction, but somehow all this—" he waved an expressive hand at the heated, happy people surrounding them—" all this seems so much more real;" and presently he found himself telling Elizabeth how he longed to retire and run a hotel, and yet could not bring himself to make the break.

" You should make up your mind to do it," she said encouragingly. " If you can afford to, why not? Rest on your past glories. Or marry Ivy and then you'd get the pub as well." She explained how Bert Higgs ran the village inn, and Harley laughed at that till his make-up threatened to run.

" I believe you're right," he said. " I believe I will retire before I'm too old to enjoy life." He shifted his position, aware once again of the constriction round his midriff.

" That's a good chap, that parson," he remarked, nodding his head towards Richard, who had at last got the field drawn up to his liking and was going down the track to the finish, leaving Bert to help Brigadier Trent start the race. Elizabeth saw how he dragged his leg as he moved, and knew how badly it must ache.

" Got a gammy leg, hasn't he?" continued Harley.

" Yes," she said. " He lost his leg during the war. He's very popular."

At that moment the field was galvanised into sudden activity as the race began, and the spectators stopped their

conversations to yell encouragement to their offspring. Forty
scampering children panted in the heat over the grass. Richard
had put the largest so far in the rear that there was no fear
of them winning, though Billy Brown sent a small girl who
was in his way flying over, and she lay sobbing in frustration
on the ground. It was hard to tell who had won in the mêlée
of waving limbs, but presently Nick, beaming from ear to ear,
appeared, led by a proud Julia who said he had come in third.
Having sorted out the victors, Richard now spoke sternly to
Billy Brown and forbade him to enter for any other race as
he had exhibited such bullying and unsportsmanlike tactics,
and such was his personality that the culprit showed real con-
trition instead of the sulkiness which was his usual reaction
to authority.

Next came an egg and spoon race, with potato eggs, and
Elizabeth went to help arrange this, for it was better to do
something active than to stand and watch Richard's limp
grow slowly worse.

XXI

No one saw Victor walking quickly down the lane. The
river wound away in the distance towards Haverstoke, and to
get over it without going on the road he must cross the field
beside the Big Meadow. It was a risk, but the crowd was pre-
occupied and the hedge between the fields was dense. He
moved quietly along, not daring to walk openly over the
middle of the field but hugging the hedge. He could hear
cheers and clapping coming from the crowd below in the
hollow, and wondered what was happening. Presently he could
distinguish the roped-off race-track and the small figures running energetically about. It was very hot and he sweated. It
must be warm work running in the races down there too. He
drew near to the marquee, which stood about twenty yards
away on the other side of the hedge. Now he must make a
dash over the open ground at this end of the field to reach the
brook, but he would still be screened by trees and bushes.
Once across the water there was an open space of pastureland

to cover before he could gain the shelter of another hedge. He had better wait till the next race was under way, so that attention would be riveted at the bottom of the field and no one would be likely to glance in his direction.

He crouched down in the shade, peering through the green hawthorn at the activity below. He could pick out Elizabeth; there she was, obviously helping in some way. He saw her speaking to Richard, then moving away down the field. Bent there, watching, he became intrigued, identifying different people he had known as the crowd surged and parted and re-arranged itself, and recognising the white-haired, soldierly figure of his father. Several races passed and still he had not moved.

Overhead once more an aeroplane zoomed through the sky, and heads turned to watch it as it spun round in a loop; looking upwards at the sky, Victor did not see Ivy come sobbing through a gap in the hedge. She recognised him at once, and put her hand to her mouth, stifling an exclamation. Then she turned quickly and ran back the way she had come.

XXII

Alan felt himself lord of the universe, seated at the controls of his aeroplane. He was alone in the heavens, master of the machine that contained him, the world a map spread out below. He swooped and swerved, singing at the top of his voice, a little mad. He had turned off his radio so that he could not hear the furious voice at the other end demanding to know why he had taken a plane up without instructions and ordering him to land at once.

He zoomed over Bramsbourne : there was the large marquee and the smaller tea tent; there was the crowd of villagers. Somewhere among that crowd was Ivy, and so were his friends Mabel and Jack who were eager to inspect her for themselves. They had been incredulous at hearing he was not coming to the Flower Show; they would be still more incredulous when they saw him overhead.

He turned steeply and looped the loop; then he roared low

over the village again and had the satisfaction of seeing faces upraised to watch him, and here and there a waving hand. He exulted. " I'll give them something to watch now," said Alan aloud. Down there was Ivy, who thought he could do nothing. Now she should see. He pointed the nose of the machine upwards and began to climb swiftly into the sky.

XXIII

Inspector Howard's men had gone through the Priory with a fine comb. Drawers and cupboards were opened, the attic stripped, every shed and outhouse searched. During all this they found the filthy suit of clothes that Elizabeth had hidden until she could destroy it.

But they found no Victor. They went methodically over the garden, and they crossed the brook and fanned out over the fields. They had a bloodhound with them, primed with the scent of Victor from his abandoned clothing. A second team spread along the road, bent on investigating every house and every possible hiding place. Not until he had searched every inch of Bramsbourne would the inspector be certain that Victor had left the neighbourhood.

It was the party in the road that Ivy met, as frightened and weeping, not knowing what to do, she ran towards her home.

XXIV

Bramsbourne gaped. It had never seen anything like the exhibition of aerobatics being given up above. The slender plane swooped and looped, spun and dived, like a soaring lark. Everyone stood and watched it, and when it turned away they found that they were breathless.

Richard's sports were delayed. He looked in annoyance at the sky; some young chap thinking he was clever, no doubt. It unnerved him too, for he had been dive-bombed and machine-gunned many times in the war and still could not feel calm with aeroplanes zooming over his head almost lifting his hair. There was still a big programme of events to be got through; the grown-ups were at this moment drawn up on the field ready for the needle-threading race, where the woman had to run carrying the thread to her partner who waited at the other end with the needle; when he had successfully threaded it both must race back to the finishing post. Richard could not get their attention; they were looking at the sky. His leg ached unbearably because he was overtired and anxious; at the back of his mind there was still the unsolved problem of Victor.

Two women looked at Richard, not the sky. One was Elizabeth, who shared his annoyance at this interruption to his hard-planned arrangements and who thought the plane flew dangerously low. The other was Mrs. Maggs; her side pained her, as it so often did now, and she felt a little sick; such hot weather did not suit her and she had found Julia and Nick surprisingly exhausting considering that the shrill voices of the young were usually music to her ears; watching them whirling round many times on the roundabout had made her quite dizzy.

Now she saw Richard, the dearest of her charges, dragging his foot along the ground and looking tense and strained; something was worrying him, she knew; he could not deceive her; wanting to borrow money this morning, for instance, as if he did not always to her knowledge have at least ten pounds in the house. He was up to something, no doubt about it, and tonight she would ferret it out of him.

Brigadier Trent growled under his breath as the roar of aeroplane engines insulted his ear-drums. "Damned young puppy, showing off, I shall report him," he grumbled.

Mabel Parkes, who found the burden of her expected child a weighty one on such a hot day, turned to her husband Jack and said, "Isn't he overdoing it a bit, Jack?"

He shaded his eyes from the sun and followed the plane as it described an arc in the sky, not answering at once.

"Is it one of our boys?" she went on anxiously.

Jack nodded. "It's one of ours all right. He isn't half showing off. I shouldn't like to be in his shoes if the C.O. hears about it."

Mabel said, " I thought no one was going up this afternoon."

" Plans must have been changed, I suppose," said Jack.

" Well, I'm glad you didn't have to, anyway," said Mabel
comfortably. She tucked her hand into his arm. " I ache, Jack.
Let's find somewhere for a sit down."

XXV

Victor too saw the antics of the aeroplane. He watched it
loop and swerve, he watched it zoom and dive. He forgot his
predicament in professional admiration of the pilot's skill. He
moved from the shelter of his field a little further into the
open, the better to see it, and stood, head back, watching.
Shining in the sun, it climbed away, then dropped like a
silent stone; it halted like a ballet dancer and circled round
in a pirouette, then turned with a roar and climbed once
more. It dived down, spinning in arabesques as it came,
twinkling in the bright light. At last it climbed again and flew
away. The crowd below relaxed and turned back to the races,
and Victor moved towards the shelter of his hedge. As he
did so, he glanced behind him, and saw something that made
his scalp prickle. In the middle distance, over the brook,
some men were crossing the field; one of them was holding
on a short leash a very large dog. Victor did not wait to con-
firm his first impression that they were policemen. He pushed
through the thick hedge into the Big Meadow and looked
wildly about him. Then he saw, entering the field by the gate
at the other side, another policeman. Frantic, he plunged into
the empty marquee which offered the nearest refuge, and
crawled under one of the tables.

XXVI

Elizabeth had forced Harley Darrell to enter the needle-
threading race as her partner. How she had managed it he
did not quite know, but here he was, ready for the fray, and
certainly their bold step into the arena had caused other more

timorous souls to follow their example and now there was a brave showing of competitors. He had taken off his jacket, which Julia kindly offered to hold, allowing one expensive sleeve to trail upon the dusty ground where presently in her excitement she hopped upon it.

Harley looked extremely nice in his dazzlingly white shirt, with his grey silk tie gleaming. Elizabeth thought he was a great sport to allow himself to be pushed into running. She stood, needle in hand, at the other end of the allotted hundred yards, with Miss Finch, the fluttering partner of that eligible widower Mr. Bert Higgs, blushing beside her. She felt sorry for Harley having to run so far after the rigours of threading the needle, and she laughed to herself, suddenly feeling incredibly happy and carefree. She was easily the first to reach the line of embarrassed men, and was still laughing while her partner fumbled with the large needle, shortsightedly missing the eye. But at last he threaded it, and raced with her up the track, soon blowing hard, but infected by her gaiety enough to try his hardest and to ignore the urgent pressure of his constricting stays. To hell with my appearance, thought Harley Darrell, seizing Elizabeth's hand and putting on a spurt; I shall not worry any more, this is the life for me; and to a burst of cheering he pulled his partner over the line first, just as the roar of an aeroplane engine again came to everyone's ears.

XXVII

Alan thought, I wonder if that's enough for her, as he turned his plane away from Bramsbourne. Then he decided, no, I'll give them one more thrill, and climbed steeply into the sky again. Five miles away he turned and dived, pointing the nose of the machine at the village, forgetting everything except that he must show his skill. Over the village he levelled out and flew slowly above the trees. Then he pulled the stick to lift the aeroplane up over the hill. Nothing happened. He tugged at it, still flying quite slowly. Still nothing happened. He could see the round white faces of the people flashing

towards him as he barely skimmed their heads, flying inevit-
ably into the hillside and the large white tent that loomed
before him.

XXVIII

Victor heard only the roar of the aircraft engines before the
world around him disintegrated. The table was blown from
above him, and as he tried to stand a huge cabbage hit him
on the head. He was half stunned, but through clouds of smoke
he could see the aeroplane buried nose first in the earth beside
him. It had torn a hole right through the marquee; half the
canvas was on the ground, the rest swayed drunkenly above
him like an Arab tent on the one pole that still stood. After
the ear-splitting noise it was queerly silent, for the engines
had cut out on the moment of impact, and the shouts and
screams from outside seemed far away. Victor was alone in the
world with a crashed aircraft that was already on fire and
might explode at any moment. His reaction was unreasoned
and instinctive; he stumbled over upturned trestles, broken
vases, onions and carrots in profuse confusion, and so at last
to the red-hot body of the machine. With little flames licking
round him, he dragged open the cockpit. Inside, the pilot
huddled, dead or unconscious, over the joystick which he still
held. It was automatic to free him; working rapidly, yet with
practised calm, Victor released his harness and managed to
pull him clear. He was dragging him away from the plane
towards a gap in the tent when the explosion came and hurled
him to the ground on top of the man he had saved.

To the watchers outside it was almost too quick to understand. One minute the plane had been flying much too low
over their heads; they watched confidently for it to rise and
clear the hill; incredulous, they saw it bury itself in the
marquee with a dull thud and a sudden silence from its
engines. There was an endless moment before frightened
screams tore the stillness, and movement returned to bodies
halted in shock. Then figures began to run towards the smok-
ing wreckage of the tent.

Richard and Harley Darrell, despite the bad leg of the one and the short breath of the other, were among the first up the hill. Jack Parke followed them, shouting to the crowd to keep away in case the fuel tanks exploded. Obediently the women fell back; Susan clasped her children and led them away in the other direction as fast as she could, and other mothers followed her example.

Time seemed to stand still in frightful silence broken only by small sounds until the explosion came. The violence of it flung Richard and Harley to the ground, but they got to their feet and went on. Flames licked round the edges of the tent and smoke poured from the hole in its top, yet fantastically half of it still stood.

Richard fought his way inside the swaying structure, and after a moment's hesitation Harley Darrell followed.

Outside the crowd, halted by the explosion, began to creep forward. Appalled, yet fascinated, they stood silently watching the place where the two men had disappeared. A few children wailed uncomprehendingly. Smoke began to pour out in huge clouds and the acrid smell of burning blew across the grass. Flames began to leap and crackle. Someone went racing off to call the fire engine, and no one thought it odd that a cordon of policemen had miraculously sprung up from nowhere to keep the crowd away. Elizabeth alone stood in front of this human chain, waiting to see if Richard would come out again.

At last through the pall of smoke two figures emerged. Between them they dragged a third, and at once willing hands went forward to their help while a ragged cheer came from the crowd. The glamorous Harley Darrell looked a very different figure now, with his hair on end and singed, a cut on his cheek where he had speared it on an upturned trestle, his clothes black and torn and burns on his hands.

Inspector Howard gently cradled the unconscious Alan against his shoulder on the ground and looked at him with an experienced eye that had witnessed the aftermath of many car smashes.

" Well, he isn't dead yet sir," he said to Richard, who also bent over him. " Badly burnt, and I should think he's smashed his head, but we'll soon have him in hospital. I suppose there wasn't another one in there too, was there?"

Richard looked at him and nodded gravely. " He'd got this chap free of the aeroplane, otherwise we couldn't have got near with the flames," he said quietly. " We dragged this man from under his body, or what was left of it. If he lives, he'll owe his life to Trent."

" You're sure it was him?"

" Certain, Inspector."

" I see," said the policeman. Then he shrugged. " Well, I suppose that's the end of one case, then, and the beginning of a new one with this pilot."

Richard peered more closely at the figure on the ground, and with a shock he recognised Alan behind the blackened features. There would be Ivy to deal with, as well as a more pressing duty. He glanced at the inspector. " Will you tell the Trents, or shall I?" he asked heavily.

" If you would prefer to do it, sir, then that's quite in order," said the inspector, and he got to his feet as, with its bell clanging, the ambulance bumped over the grass towards them.

EPILOGUE

On an evening in September Mrs. Trent came into the drawing-room through the french window, carrying a dozen or so roses. Behind her in the garden long late summer shadows slanted over the grass, and the borders were full of crimson and blue michaelmas daisies.

"Look, George, aren't these lovely?" she said, sniffing the flowers she held. "They've been wonderful this year. I thought they'd be so nice in Elizabeth's room."

Brigadier Trent looked up from *The Time*s and peered at the roses over the top of his spectacles. "I never remember them doing so well," he agreed, and returned to his reading.

His wife went through the house to fetch a vase. When she had put the roses in water she took them upstairs. The window in Elizabeth's small room was open, and she paused to gaze from it for a moment; in the distance the hill was white now with stubble, except for a few patches of grass. Hedges and trees were dark with the heavy green preceding their fading.

Elizabeth's brushes were on the dressing-table; a cardigan, neatly folded, lay on the chair; blue bedroom slippers were below it. Elizabeth had come home.

Downstairs again, Mrs. Trent glanced through the picture paper. Then she exclaimed, "Have you seen this, George? Harley Darrell is retiring from the films!"

"Sensible fellow," grunted the Brigadier.

Mrs. Trent was reading aloud. Snatches came to him: "Press conference today—decided to retire before too old—plans to open hotel on the Thames—peace and quiet of country life—recent experiences." She put the paper down. "Well, I am surprised," she said.

"He's got some sense, that chap," said her husband. "And some guts, what's more."

Both were silent then, remembering the accident.

"Though he only followed where Richard led," went on the Brigadier.

"Still, he did follow, he might have stayed behind," she reminded him. "And Richard could never have got that foolish boy out alone."

"I suppose not." Brigadier Trent sat staring into space. "It's extraordinary how long ago it seems, yet it's only six weeks."

"I know." Involuntarily Mrs. Trent's eyes turned towards her desk, where now the photograph of Victor in his R.A.F. uniform stood once more.

"The boy had some guts too, in the end," said the Brigadier, subconsciously following her thought. "That makes it easier, somehow."

"Yes, dear," she said gently. Poor George; it was difficult for him to grow used to feeling proud of Victor again. Every so often he uttered small remarks like this which showed the process was developing; he made conscious efforts to speak about his son, remembering childish exploits and bringing him back once more from the limbo of his banishment. Mrs. Trent understood how hard it was to adjust to these new feelings; she realised too how terrible the shock had been for him that Monday evening when Richard, burnt and blackened, had told them what had happened in the wrecked marquee.

For herself, after the first grief and dismay, it had been easier. Gradually she began to feel that Victor's ceaseless struggle against life had ended in peace. If he had lived, what would have become of him? He could never have accepted the limits of society; as time went on he would have got more desperate, more cunning, more alone. Now he was beyond all that; and in the manner of his death he had vindicated himself. No, though sometimes she still wept secretly for her child, Mrs. Trent was not sad.

"That airman, young Blake," said the Brigadier now, becoming practical. "Have you heard how he's getting on?"

"Yes, indeed," she told him. "I've been to see him. Poor boy, his family live too far away to make the journey and I felt so sorry for him. He is being discharged from hospital next week, though of course he still needs crutches, and I'm afraid it will be months before he's really well."

"I wonder what they'll do to him," mused the Brigadier.

"His court martial is coming up very soon," said Mrs. Trent. "He thinks he will be dismissed the service."

"Good Lord, will he? Yes, I suppose he couldn't have done much worse," said the Brigadier.

"And all to impress that silly Ivy," she said. "He told me how it had happened." She related what Alan, lying miserably in his hospital bed, had told her.

The Brigadier's only answer was a groan.

"Well, one good thing is that Ivy's come to her senses," said Mrs. Trent more cheerfully. "And whatever happens to Alan, she intends to marry him. Silly girl, she wouldn't go and see him in hospital until I made her, but then they arranged it all."

"You seem to have been very busy, Marjorie. I had no idea you were doing all this," said the Brigadier in some surprise.

"Well, dear, I didn't mention it as I wasn't sure how you'd feel about it," she said. "But I felt we owed it to Victor to see that Alan was all right. And Elizabeth asked me to talk to Ivy."

"Quite right to help the boy," approved the Brigadier. "If he is dismissed, we might see what we can do to find him a decent job."

"Yes dear," Mrs. Trent agreed. Then, after a little pause, she said, "Did you know that Alan's friend, that other airman who was so splendid after the accident, is calling his son Harley? Or rather I should say it's his wife's idea. Ivy told me; she goes to see them often. The baby was born that night, a little earlier than expected. Ivy was rather amusing about it, she didn't think it at all a good idea."

"Neither do I," said her husband. "What an awful name to saddle an innocent child with."

"Well, he's thriving, and that's what really matters," said Mrs. Trent. She looked at her watch. "Goodness, I had no idea it was so late, it's nearly seven o'clock. I must go and tidy."

"I thought Richard was coming to dinner," said the Brigadier.

"He is; he'll be here soon, I expect," said Mrs. Trent.

"Where's Elizabeth got to? I've hardly seen her since she arrived," he complained.

Mrs. Trent paused at the door and smiled. "I think she's gone down to the brook to meet him," she said, and went from the room leaving her husband to absorb a wholly new idea.

Elizabeth and Richard were leaning on the bridge watching the clear water flowing past underneath. They were silent for a time, until Elizabeth suddenly gave a deep, contented sigh.

Richard smiled then, and asked, "Happy?"

She nodded.

"You heaved such a great sigh," he said.

"It's so wonderful to think I needn't leave this time," she said. "Richard, is it very wicked of me to be so happy when such terrible things have happened?"

"I think a little happiness was owing to you," he said gently.

"It was awful at first," she remembered. "I kept thinking it was all my fault, that dreadful night. We all thought he had got away safely, and then you told us, and all on top of you getting burnt like that."

Richard waited for her to go on. Her hand rested on the rail of the bridge, and he put his own bandaged one over it.

"But after a while," she continued, "I began to think, supposing he had spent most of his life in and out of gaol, which might have happened, until perhaps he died in some other dreadful circumstances—robbery with violence, or something like that. This way was better."

"He was very brave," said Richard.

"Yes. And he must have been so frightened, with the police almost on top of him, before the crash."

"It must have all happened very quickly," Richard said. "He couldn't have felt any pain."

She nodded again. Then she said, "One of the good things is that his parents can be proud again. Father speaks about him every day."

"He has good reason for pride now," said Richard.

They were silent again, hands loosely linked.

"How long will the Trents need you, Beth?" he asked her then.

Elizabeth turned to face him, and said, a little breathlessly, "I don't know."

"I need you too, my darling," he said.

At last she smiled, and colour filled her face. Richard looked at her very tenderly, and then he kissed her.

Presently, hand in hand, they walked slowly up the shadowed garden and into the house together.